I0782105

The Blackstone Alliance

Book 1: The Formation

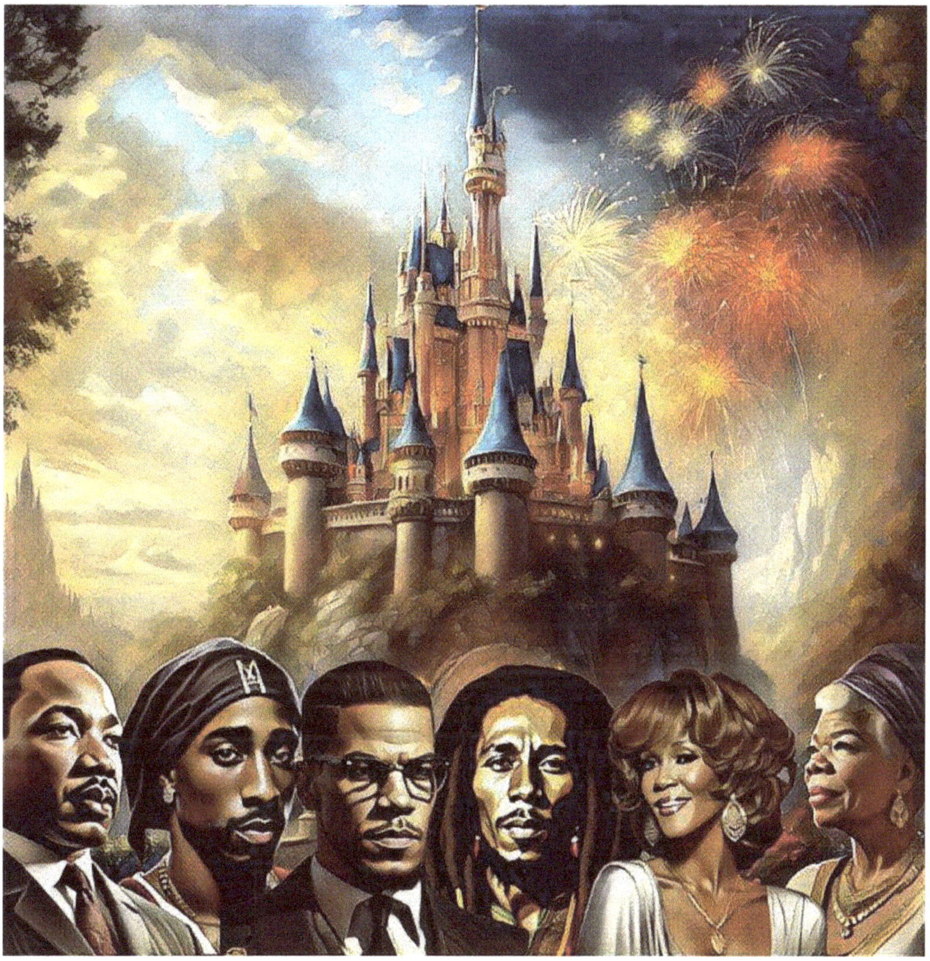

By Karajah Yashar

Orlando, FL 2024

The Blackstone Alliance is Historical/ Futuristic Fiction

In the vast genre of historical fiction, there exists a subgenre that weaves together the threads of fact and imagination, bringing to life the figures who have shaped our past. This is the realm of fiction utilizing real historical figures—a realm where the boundaries between history and storytelling blur, and where the lives of the celebrated and the unsung become intertwined with the fabric of fiction.

In these stories, real historical figures step off the pages of history books and into the realm of fiction, where they find themselves embroiled in the dramas, conflicts, and triumphs of imagined narratives. From kings and queens to artists and revolutionaries, these figures become characters in their own right, navigating the twists and turns of fictional plotlines while retaining the essence of their historical personas.

Yet, while these stories may be fictional, they are grounded in the rich tapestry of cultural conditions, drawing upon real places, contexts, and personalities to create a vivid and immersive world. The author has meticulously researched the lives of these historical figures, striving to capture their voices, motivations, and impact on the world with authenticity and respect.

Through fiction utilizing real historical figures, readers are transported to different dimensions, gaining insight into the complexities of the human experience across time and space. These stories offer a tantalizing blend of history and imagination, inviting readers to explore figures of the past through modern eyes and to ponder the timeless questions that continue to resonate in the present.

So, dear reader, journey with us into the realm of fiction utilizing real historical figures, where the future comes alive in all its richness, complexity, and intrigue. Together, let us embark on a voyage with historical icons, where the boundaries between fact and fiction blur, and where the people of the past become windows into the human soul.

The 2040 A.D. Apocalypse

The year is 2040 AD, humanity finds itself teetering on the brink of an unprecedented apocalypse—a cataclysmic convergence of ecological collapse, technological upheaval, and geopolitical strife that threatens to unravel the very fabric of civilization.

As the world reels from a series of devastating natural disasters: superstorms ravage coastal cities, wildfires consume vast swaths of land, earthquakes shake up buildings in divers places, and droughts parch once-fertile regions into arid wastelands. Rising sea levels inundate low-lying areas, displacing millions and triggering waves of refugees fleeing environmental catastrophe.

Meanwhile, advances in artificial intelligence and automation have ushered in a new era of technological disruption, reshaping economies and societies in unforeseen ways. Massive job losses lead to widespread social unrest, as automation replaces human labor at an unprecedented pace, leaving millions without means of livelihood.

Amidst this turmoil, geopolitical tensions escalate to the breaking point, as nations vie for dwindling resources and strategic advantage in a world gripped by chaos and uncertainty. Proxy conflicts erupt into full-scale warfare, unleashing untold suffering and devastation on a global scale.

As the situation grows increasingly dire, voices of dissent rise up against the ruling powers, demanding change and accountability in the face of looming catastrophe. But their pleas fall on deaf ears, as entrenched interests cling to power and refuse to acknowledge the gravity of the situation.

In the midst of this turmoil, whispers of ancient prophecies and apocalyptic visions echo through the collective consciousness, warning of an impending reckoning—a final judgment that will sweep away the old order and herald the dawn of a new era. Some see hope in these prophecies, viewing them as a chance for renewal and transformation amidst the chaos. Others dismiss them as mere superstition, clinging to the belief that humanity can still avert disaster through ingenuity and perseverance.

The Orlando Florida Race Riots

In the heart of Orlando, Florida, a city known for its vibrant culture and diverse communities, tensions simmer beneath the surface, threatening to erupt into chaos and conflict. Against the backdrop of social inequality and simmering resentment, a series of events ignite the powder keg, plunging the city into a race riot unlike any it has ever seen.

It begins with a tragic incident—an unarmed Black teenager is shot and killed by a police officer under disputed circumstances. The news spreads like wildfire on social media, fueling outrage and indignation among the city's Black community, who see yet another instance of systemic injustice and police brutality.

As protests erupt in the streets, demanding justice for the slain teenager, tensions between the Black community and law enforcement reach a boiling point. Scenes of unrest and violence unfold as clashes break out between protesters and police, with tear gas and rubber bullets filling the air.

But the unrest does not stop there. As news of the shooting spreads, long-standing grievances and resentments between Orlando's Black and white communities bubble to the surface, exacerbated by economic inequality, racial profiling, and a history of segregation and discrimination.

Amidst the chaos, rumors and misinformation spread like wildfire, stoking fear and paranoia on all sides. Social media platforms become battlegrounds for competing narratives, with inflammatory rhetoric and conspiracy theories fueling the flames of division and mistrust.

Caught in the crossfire are ordinary residents of Orlando, who find themselves torn between loyalty to their community and a desire for peace and reconciliation. Businesses are vandalized, homes are damaged, and lives are shattered as the city descends into chaos and lawlessness.

Birth of the Blackstones

As the civil unrest grows, a group of young black activists storm the theme park's Mystic Kingdom. Upon entering, they plead to God for the wisdom and courage of their ancestors, who courageously fought oppression. As they sat in the theme park's Castle, one young man angrily kicks a vase containing a blue liquid and suddenly, a phenomenon unlike any other unfolds. With a crackle of cosmic energy, a mysterious portal materializes, shimmering with an otherworldly glow that captivates all who behold it. From within this shimmering gateway, six figures of legend and lore emerge, stepping forth into the modern world with a sense of wonder and bewilderment.

Out of this newly formed portal, Malcolm X, Tupac Shakur, Maya Angelou, Whitney Houston, Martin Luther King Jr., and Bob Marley found themselves resurrected as immortals, their essence woven into the fabric of eternity.

As they emerged from the depths of the timeless abyss, they found themselves standing in a surreal landscape bathed in a gentle glow. Their eyes, once veiled by mortal limitations, now beheld the vastness of existence with clarity beyond comprehension.

Malcolm X, his voice resonating with unwavering conviction, spoke first. "We are given a chance beyond the grasp of mortal understanding. Let us use our newfound immortality to ignite the flames of change once more."

Tupac Shakur, the lyrical prophet of the streets, nodded in agreement. "Our words are our weapons, and our actions are our legacy. Let us carve a path of righteousness through the annals of time."

Maya Angelou, her presence exuding wisdom and grace, smiled softly. "In the tapestry of existence, let our voices sing of hope and resilience. Let us be the guiding stars for those who seek light in the darkness."

Whitney Houston, her voice a celestial melody, added, "Let our songs be the anthem of unity and love, echoing through the corridors of eternity."

Martin Luther King Jr., his spirit undimmed by the passage of time, raised his fist in solidarity. "Let justice be our compass, and compassion be our guiding light. Together, we shall overcome."

Bob Marley, his soul pulsating with the rhythms of rebellion, nodded in agreement. "Let us spread the message of peace and harmony, for in unity, there is strength."

And so, the six immortals embarked on their journey, traversing through the realms of existence, leaving trails of enlightenment and inspiration in their wake. They stood against injustice, sang of freedom, and danced in the eternal rhythms of love.

Their legacy transcended the boundaries of mortal comprehension, for they were not mere mortals bound by time, but immortal spirits bound by the threads of destiny. And as they journeyed through the ages, their voices echoed through eternity, a testament to the enduring power of the human spirit.

As the specter of a race war looms on the horizon, casting its shadow over the hearts and minds of humanity, these luminaries come together with a shared purpose—to lend their voices, their wisdom, and their collective strength to the cause of justice and reconciliation. They form an alliance like no other, a brotherhood and sisterhood forged in the crucible of adversity, bound together by a common struggle and a shared vision of a better world.

They call themselves **Blackstone Alliance**—an unbreakable partnership of souls united in the fight against injustice and oppression, a beacon of hope in a world shrouded in darkness. With Malcolm X as their guiding light, they chart a course of action, blending the tactics of resistance with the power of dialogue and diplomacy. Tupac Shakur, with his gift for words and his unyielding spirit, rallies the masses with his impassioned pleas for unity and solidarity. Maya Angelou, with her wisdom and insight, offers counsel and guidance, urging patience and perseverance in the face of adversity.

Whitney Houston, with her angelic voice and her boundless compassion, spreads a message of love and healing, soothing the wounds of a fractured society. Martin Luther King Jr., with his vision of a beloved community, inspires hope and courage in the hearts of all who hear his words. And Bob Marley, with his music and his message of redemption, rallies the forces of righteousness to stand firm against the tide of hatred and division.

Together, they stand as beacons of light in a world engulfed by darkness, leading the way forward with courage, conviction, and unwavering faith in the power of love to overcome hate. For in the heart of every human soul, they whisper, lies the seed of redemption—a seed that, when nurtured with compassion and understanding, has the power to transform the world and usher in a new era of peace, justice, and equality for their people.

Malcolm X Gives a Speech

In the heart of a bustling city, amidst a throng of eager listeners, Malcolm X stands tall, his presence commanding attention as he prepares to deliver a speech that will reverberate through the corridors of history. With a steely gaze and a voice that resonates with power and conviction, he begins to address the crowd, igniting a flame of passion and determination in the hearts of all who hear his words.

"My brothers and sisters," Malcolm begins, his voice cutting through the din of the crowd, "we stand here today at a crossroads—a moment of reckoning for our people and our nation. For too long, we have been shackled by the chains of oppression, denied the rights and freedoms that are our birthright as human beings. But I say to you now, the time for complacency is over. The time for silence is past. The time to rise up and demand justice is now!"

As Malcolm speaks, his words ring out like thunder, electrifying the air with their power and resonance. He speaks of the injustices faced by the Black community—the systemic racism, the economic exploitation, the violence and discrimination that have plagued their lives for generations. But he also speaks of hope—a hope born from the resilience and determination of a people who refuse to be silenced, who refuse to accept the status quo.

"We must be willing to fight for our rights," Malcolm declares, his voice rising with passion. "We must be willing to stand up and demand equality, dignity, and respect. We must be willing to challenge the powers that seek to oppress us, to tear down the walls of prejudice and injustice that divide us. For we are not alone in this struggle. We stand united, a mighty force for change, determined to break the chains of bondage and claim our rightful place in the world."

As Malcolm's speech reaches its crescendo, the crowd erupts into cheers and applause, their hearts ablaze with the fire of revolution. Inspired by his words, they pledge themselves to the cause of justice, vowing to stand firm in the face of adversity and oppression. For in Malcolm X, they see not just a leader, but a beacon of hope—a voice of truth and courage in a world hungry for change.

And as the echoes of his speech fade into the night, the spirit of resistance burns ever brighter in the hearts of the Black community, fueled by the passion and determination ignited by Malcolm's words. For they know that as long as they stand together, united in purpose and vision, they will never be silenced, and their voices will ring out for justice, equality, and freedom for all.

Malcolm X Speech Inspires Tupac

In the dimly lit room of a crowded apartment, Tupac Shakur sits transfixed, his eyes fixed on the flickering screen before him. The words of Malcolm X echo through the small space, filling the air with their power and resonance, and Tupac feels a fire ignite within him—a fire of passion and purpose that he knows will burn long after the speech has ended.

As Malcolm speaks of the struggles and injustices faced by the Black community, Tupac nods in silent agreement, his heart swelling with admiration for the man whose words resonate so deeply with his own beliefs and convictions. He sees in Malcolm X a kindred spirit—a warrior for justice and equality, unafraid to speak truth to power and challenge the status quo.

"Damn, that's real," Tupac mutters to himself, his voice barely above a whisper. "That's the truth right there."

As the speech reaches its climax, Tupac feels a surge of emotion welling up inside him—a mix of anger, determination, and hope. Inspired by Malcolm's words, he knows that he must do more than just listen—he must act. He must use his own voice and platform to speak out against injustice, to shine a light on the struggles of his people, and to fight for a better world for future generations.

And so, as the echoes of Malcolm's speech fade into the night, Tupac rises from his seat with a newfound sense of purpose. He knows that the road ahead will be long and difficult, filled with obstacles and challenges at every turn. But he also knows that as long as he stands firm in his convictions, as long as he refuses to be silenced or deterred, he can make a difference. He can be a force for change—a voice of truth and inspiration in a world hungry for justice and equality.

And with that thought burning bright in his mind, Tupac sets out into the night, ready to take on whatever challenges may come his way, fueled by the fire of Malcolm X's speech and the unwavering belief that together, they can create a world where all are truly free.

Tupac Meets with Maya Angelou and Malcolm X

As the light of day begins to peak through an Orlando community leader's home, three iconic figures sit with him in solemn contemplation, their presence commanding attention as they prepare to discuss the future of their people. Malcolm X, with his steely gaze and unwavering resolve, sits at the head of the table, his focus on instilling discipline and self-respect within the Black community. Maya Angelou, the voice of wisdom and grace, sits beside him, her gentle demeanor belying a fierce determination to educate and empower their people. And Tupac Shakur, the poet laureate of the streets, leans forward with intensity, his mind already racing with plans to unite and protect their community.

"Brothers and sisters," Malcolm begins, his voice cutting through the silence like a thunderclap. "We stand at a crossroads—a moment of reckoning for our people. We must be disciplined, focused, and unwavering in our commitment to uplift ourselves and each other. We cannot afford to be divided or distracted by petty rivalries or internal strife. We must stand as one, united in purpose and vision."

Maya nods in agreement, her eyes shining with determination. "Education is key," she adds, her voice soft but resolute. "We must arm our people with knowledge and wisdom, empowering them to think critically, question authority, and chart their own path to liberation. Education is the great equalizer—the weapon with which we can defeat ignorance and prejudice."

Tupac leans back in his chair, his mind already spinning with ideas. "And what about protection?" he interjects, his voice tinged with urgency. "We can't just sit back and wait for change to come. We need to be proactive—we need to arm ourselves and protect our communities from those who seek to harm us. And we need to reach out to our brothers and sisters in the streets, to the gang members and the hustlers, and show them that there's more to life than violence and crime towards each other. We need to unite them, empower them, and give them a sense of purpose and belonging."

Malcolm and Maya exchange a knowing glance, recognizing the truth in Tupac's words. "Unity is our greatest strength," Malcolm declares, his voice filled with conviction. "We must come together as a community, setting aside our differences and standing shoulder to shoulder in the fight for justice and equality. Only then can we truly achieve liberation—for ourselves, for our children, and for generations to come."

With their plan set and their resolve firm, the three legendary figures rise from the table, ready to embark on their mission to revolutionize their community. For Malcolm X, Maya Angelou, and Tupac Shakur, the journey ahead will be long and arduous, filled with obstacles and challenges at every turn. But with discipline, education, and unity as their guiding principles, they know that they can overcome any obstacle and achieve their vision of a brighter future for their people.

Tupac Meets with Bob Marley

In a secluded corner of a bustling city, Tupac Shakur and Bob Marley sit in a vegan restaurant in downtown Orlando, their voices mingling with the gentle sound of traffic noise outside, as they discuss the future of their people. Tupac, with his intensity and passion, speaks of revolution in the language of the streets—of guns, gangs, and uniting the hood against oppression. Bob Marley, with his calm and spiritual presence, offers a different perspective, speaking of a revolution of the soul—a spiritual awakening that transcends the boundaries of race, class, and creed.

"Tupac, my brother," Bob begins, his voice low and melodious. "I hear your words, and I understand your anger and frustration. But violence only begets more violence. We cannot fight fire with fire—we must fight hate with love, darkness with light. The true revolution, my friend, is not fought with guns and fists, but with kindness, compassion, and understanding."

Tupac nods, his brow furrowed in thought. "I hear you, Bob," he replies, his voice tinged with uncertainty. "But how do we fight back against the forces that seek to oppress us? How do we protect ourselves and our communities from violence and injustice?"

Bob smiles gently, his eyes shining with wisdom. "We fight back with the most powerful weapon of all—our spirit," he says. "We must rise above the hatred and division that seek to tear us apart, and embrace the power of love and unity. We must come together as brothers and sisters, bound by a common purpose and a shared vision of a better world for all."

Tupac listens intently, his mind racing with possibilities. "So you're saying we need a spiritual revolution?" he asks, his voice tinged with skepticism.

Bob nods, his smile widening. "Yes, my brother. A revolution of the heart—a revolution that begins within each and every one of us. For only when we heal the wounds of the past and open our hearts to love and forgiveness can we truly create a world of peace, justice, and equality."

As the sun sets on their conversation, Tupac and Bob rise from their seats, their hearts lighter and their minds clearer. Though their paths may diverge, they know that they share a common goal—to uplift and empower their people, to fight for justice and equality, and to leave behind a legacy of hope and inspiration for future generations. And with that shared vision burning bright in their souls, they set out into the world, ready to embark on their respective journeys of revolution—one armed with guns, the other armed with music, but both united in their quest for a better tomorrow.

Bob Marley Tells Whitney Houston about Tupac's Plans

In a quiet corner of the humming city, Bob Marley finds Whitney Houston sitting alone, her eyes bright and hopeful. Sensing her positive vibes, Bob approaches her with a gentle smile, his voice soft and soothing. They share a few laughs, then Bob Marley starts to talk about his conversation with Tupac.

"Whitney, my sister," he begins, "I've heard disturbing news about Tupac's plans for the hood. He talks of uniting gang members and inciting a violent revolution."

Whitney's eyes widen in alarm, her heart heavy with concern. "That sounds dangerous, Bob," she replies, her voice tinged with apprehension. "Violence only begets more violence. We can't fight hate with hate—we have to find another way."

Bob nods in agreement, his expression grave. "You're right, Whitney. Violence is never the answer. We must seek a path of peace and reconciliation, not one of bloodshed and destruction."

"But how do we stop Tupac?" Whitney asks, her voice trembling with worry.

"We talk to him," Bob replies, his voice firm but gentle. "We remind him of the power of love and unity, of the importance of building bridges, not walls. We show him that there is another way—a way that leads to healing and hope, not despair and destruction."

Whitney nods, her heart heavy with resolve. "I'll talk to him, Bob," she says, her voice steady despite her fear. "I'll remind him of the strength that lies in unity, the beauty that lies in diversity, and the power of music to heal and inspire."

As they part ways, Whitney feels a sense of determination coursing through her veins. She knows that the road ahead will be difficult, filled with challenges and obstacles at every turn. But she also knows that she cannot stand idly by while her brothers and sisters are led astray by the false promise of violence and revenge.

At the end of their conversation, Bob and Whitney agree to get together and perform at a unity concert where they will promote love and reconciliation. This will help unite the people of Orlando.

Armed with the power of love and the strength of her convictions, Whitney sets out to confront Tupac, to show him that there is another way—a way that leads to peace, justice, and a brighter tomorrow for all. And with Bob's words of wisdom echoing in her mind, she knows that she is not alone in her quest—that together, they can change the course of history and build a better world for future generations.

Whitney Houston Meets with Tupac Shakur

In a large room in Tupac's Condo, Whitney Houston and Tupac Shakur sit facing each other, the tension palpable in the air between them. Whitney's eyes reflect a mixture of concern and determination, while Tupac's demeanor exudes a sense of urgency and defiance. They are on opposite sides of the table, figuratively and literally, as they engage in a dialogue about revolution with guns.

"Tupac, I understand your frustration and your desire for change," Whitney begins, her voice measured but firm. "But I can't condone violence as a means to achieve it. We can't fight fire with fire—it only leads to more destruction and suffering."

Tupac leans forward, his eyes flashing with intensity. "Whitney, you don't get it," he retorts, his voice tinged with frustration. "We can't just sit back and wait for change to come. Sometimes, you gotta fight for what you believe in, even if it means getting your hands dirty."

"But at what cost, Tupac?" Whitney counters, her voice rising with emotion. "Violence only breeds more violence. It tears families apart, destroys communities, and perpetuates a cycle of pain and suffering that never ends. We have to find another way—a way that leads to healing and reconciliation, not more bloodshed and heartache."

Tupac shakes his head, his resolve unwavering. "I hear you, Whitney, but you don't know what it's like out there," he says, his voice tinged with bitterness. "You don't know what it's like to grow up in the hood, surrounded by poverty, crime, and violence every day. Sometimes, you gotta fight just to survive."

Whitney sighs, her heart heavy with sorrow. "I may not know your pain, Tupac, but I know that violence is never the answer," she says, her voice soft but resolute. "We have to rise above our circumstances, to break the cycle of violence and despair, and to build a better future for ourselves and our children."

As their dialogue comes to an impasse, Whitney and Tupac find themselves at odds, unable to bridge the gap between their perspectives. They may not come to an agreement in this moment, but their conversation serves as a reminder of the complexity and urgency of the issues they face—and of the need for dialogue, understanding, and compassion in the pursuit of justice and equality.

Whitney Goes to See Dr. Martin Luther King Jr.

In a brightly lit Jamaican restaurant in the Pine Hills section of Orlando, Whitney Houston seeks out the wisdom and guidance of a towering figure in the struggle for justice and equality—Martin Luther King Jr. She finds him sitting in contemplation, his demeanor serene yet resolute, his presence exuding a sense of quiet strength and unwavering conviction.

"Dr. King, I need your help," Whitney begins, her voice trembling with concern. "Tupac is planning a violent revolution, and I don't know what to do. I know that violence is never the answer, but I'm afraid that if I keep confronting him, he'll just push me away."

Dr. King listens attentively, his eyes filled with compassion and understanding. "Whitney, my dear sister, I understand your fear and your frustration," he replies, his voice calm and reassuring. "But violence only begets more violence. We cannot build a better world by tearing down others—it must be built on a foundation of love, compassion, and understanding."

Whitney nods, her heart heavy with relief. "I know that, Dr. King," she says, her voice tinged with gratitude. "But how do I convince Tupac? How do I show him that there is another way—a way that leads to peace and justice for all?"

Dr. King smiles gently, his eyes shining with wisdom. "You speak to his heart, Whitney," he replies, his voice filled with conviction. "You show him that the path of nonviolence is not just the right thing to do—it is the only thing to do. You remind him of the power of love to heal, to transform, and to bring about real and lasting change."

As their conversation continues, Whitney feels a sense of peace and clarity wash over her. She knows that the road ahead will be difficult, filled with challenges and obstacles at every turn. But she also knows that she is not alone—that Dr. King's words of wisdom and guidance will be her North Star, guiding her on her journey to confront Tupac and show him that there is another way—a way of peace, justice, and love for all.

Whitney Houston Meets with Malcolm X

In a quiet room in Malcolm X's downtown Orlando office, Whitney Houston sits across from Malcolm X, her heart heavy with concern as she shares her worries about Tupac's plans for a violent revolution. Malcolm X listens attentively, his expression serious yet contemplative, as he considers her words.

"Whitney, I understand your apprehension," Malcolm begins, his voice measured but firm. "Violence is never an ideal solution, but sometimes it's a necessary one. Tupac's idea of uniting gang members may seem radical, but it has the potential to strike fear in the oppressor and demonstrate our collective strength."

Whitney's eyes widen in surprise, her heart sinking at Malcolm's response. "But Malcolm, violence only begets more violence," she counters, her voice tinged with desperation. "We can't fight hate with hate—we have to find another way. We have to show the world that we're better than that, that we're capable of rising above our circumstances and building a better future for ourselves and our children."

Malcolm nods, his expression thoughtful. "You're right, Whitney. Violence is a double-edged sword, and it often leads to unintended consequences. But sometimes, when all other avenues have been exhausted, it's the only option we have left."

As their conversation comes to a close, Whitney feels a sense of disappointment weighing heavily on her heart. She had hoped that Malcolm would share her conviction that violence is never the answer, but she understands that he sees things from a different perspective—a perspective shaped by his own experiences and beliefs.

As she leaves the room, Whitney knows that she must continue to stand firm in her commitment to nonviolence, even in the face of opposition. She may not be able to change Malcolm's mind, but she can stay true to her own convictions and work towards a future where peace, justice, and equality reign supreme.

Maya Angelou and Tupac Discuss Youth Education and Defense

In a sunlit library adorned with vibrant artwork, Maya Angelou and Tupac Shakur engage in a dialogue about the education of youth. Maya, with her gentle yet commanding presence, emphasizes the importance of the arts as a tool for empowerment and expression, while Tupac, fueled by his own experiences, advocates for self-defense as a means of survival and empowerment.

"Maya, my dear sister," Tupac begins, his voice filled with respect, "I understand the power of the arts, but in the streets where I come from, survival is the priority. We need to teach our youth how to defend themselves against the violence and oppression that surrounds them."

Maya nods, her eyes filled with understanding. "I hear you, Tupac," she replies, her voice soft but resolute. "But we must also recognize the transformative power of the arts. Through music, poetry, dance, and visual arts, we can inspire hope, cultivate creativity, and foster a sense of belonging and purpose in our youth."

Tupac considers Maya's words, his expression thoughtful. "I see what you're saying, Maya," he responds, his voice tinged with admiration. "But how do we strike a balance between artistic expression and self-defense? How do we ensure that our youth have the tools they need to navigate the challenges they face while also nurturing their creativity and potential?"

Maya smiles gently, her wisdom shining through. "It's about providing our youth with a comprehensive education—one that encompasses not only the arts but also practical skills and knowledge," she explains. "We can teach them self-defense techniques to protect themselves physically, while also nurturing their artistic talents to empower them emotionally and spiritually."

As their conversation continues, Maya and Tupac find common ground in their shared commitment to empowering youth. While they may approach the issue from different perspectives, they both recognize the importance of providing young people with the tools and resources they need to thrive in a world that can often be harsh and unforgiving.

As they part ways, Maya and Tupac feel a sense of optimism and determination coursing through their veins. They know that by working together, they can create a future where all youth have the opportunity to reach their full potential, armed with both the skills to defend themselves and the creativity to inspire change.

Bob Marley Discusses Marijuana Use With Malcolm X

In a serene setting, amidst the calming rhythms of nature, Bob Marley and Malcolm X engage in a spirited debate about marijuana use in their community. Bob, with his easygoing demeanor and deep reverence for the herb, argues passionately in favor of its benefits, while Malcolm, with his stern resolve and commitment to upliftment, voices his concerns about its potential negative impact.

"Bob, my brother," Malcolm begins, his voice measured but firm, "I understand that you see marijuana as a sacred herb, but we must consider its effects on our community. It can lead to addiction, apathy, and a lack of productivity—things that we can ill afford in our struggle for liberation and empowerment."

Bob nods, his expression thoughtful. "I hear you, Malcolm," he replies, his voice tinged with respect. "But I also believe that marijuana has the power to heal, to inspire, and to bring people together. It's been used for centuries as a medicine, a sacrament, and a source of creativity and spiritual enlightenment."

Malcolm considers Bob's words, his brow furrowed in thought. "I understand your perspective, Bob, but we must be mindful of the consequences of promoting drug use, even Marijuana, in our community," he says, his voice tinged with concern. "We need our people to be clear-headed, focused, and determined in our fight for justice and equality."

Bob Marley nods thoughtfully at Malcolm X's concerns about marijuana addiction. His easy smile softens as he considers the gravity of the issue, recognizing the potential harm that addiction can bring to individuals and communities alike.

"Malcolm, my brother," Bob begins, his voice calm and measured, "I hear your concerns about addiction, and I agree that it's a serious issue that we can't ignore. Perhaps we should focus our efforts on providing addiction counseling and support for those in our community who are struggling with substance abuse problems, whether it's marijuana or any other substance."

Malcolm's expression softens as he senses Bob's sincerity and willingness to address the issue head-on. "I appreciate your openness to finding solutions, Bob," he replies, his voice reflecting a sense of relief. "Addiction affects us all, and it's important that we come together as a community to support those who are struggling and help them find the resources and assistance they need to overcome their challenges."

As they continue their conversation, Bob and Malcolm find common ground in their commitment to addressing the root causes of addiction and providing support and guidance to those in need. They recognize that while marijuana may have its benefits, such as in teas, it's essential to approach its use with caution and mindfulness, especially for those who may be vulnerable to substance abuse and addiction.

With their shared determination to uplift and empower their community, Bob and Malcolm set out to work together, drawing on their strengths and resources to create a future where everyone has the opportunity to live healthy, fulfilling lives free from the grip of addiction. And as they join forces, they know that their combined efforts will make a meaningful difference in the lives of those who need it most.

Tupac Meets to Unite Rival Gang Members

In the heart of the city, amidst the shadows of towering buildings and the hum of urban life, Tupac Shakur meets with rival gang members in a tense yet hopeful gathering. With determination in his eyes and passion in his voice, Tupac lays out his vision for unity and solidarity in the face of oppression and injustice.

"My brothers," Tupac begins, his voice carrying the weight of his convictions, "we may come from different gangs, but we share a common enemy—the system that seeks to keep us down, to divide us, and to strip away our dignity and humanity. But if we stand together, if we unite as one, we can't be stopped. We can change the world."

The gang members exchange wary glances, their expressions guarded yet curious. They've been taught to distrust each other, to see their rivals as enemies to be feared and avoided. But there's something about Tupac's words, something in the fire of his passion and the sincerity of his conviction, that resonates with them.

"We've been fighting each other for too long," Tupac continues, his voice tinged with urgency. "But imagine what we could accomplish if we put aside our differences and focused our energy on fighting the real enemy—the system that keeps us trapped in poverty, violence, and despair. Together, we can make a difference. Together, we can change the world."

Slowly, hesitantly, the gang members begin to nod in agreement, their eyes lighting up with a newfound sense of purpose and possibility. They may not trust each other completely, but they recognize the truth in Tupac's words—the power of unity, the strength of solidarity, and the potential for change when people come together for a common cause.

And as they shake hands and exchange nods of solidarity, Tupac and the rival gang members know that this is just the beginning of their journey—a journey of transformation, of resistance, and of revolution. Together, they will stand as one, united in their determination to fight for justice, equality, and freedom for all. And with Tupac leading the way, they know that anything is possible. Tupac concluded the meeting by saying *"We gotta make a change. It's time for us as a people to start makin' some changes. Let's change the way we eat, let's change the way we live. And let's change the way we treat each other. You see, the old way wasn't working. So it's on us to do what we gotta do, to survive."*

Whitney Houston Meets with Tupac and Some Gang Leaders

In a room filled with anticipation and excitement, Whitney Houston sits down with Tupac Shakur and a group of gang members to discuss an upcoming unity concert that she is organizing alongside Bob Marley. The atmosphere is charged with energy as Whitney shares her vision for the event—a celebration of unity, peace, and solidarity in the face of adversity.

"My friends," Whitney begins, her voice ringing out with passion and determination, "we have the opportunity to come together as a community, to stand side by side in solidarity and defiance against the forces that seek to divide us. This concert is more than just music—it's a symbol of hope, a beacon of light in the darkness, and a testament to the power of unity."

Tupac nods in agreement, his eyes shining with excitement. "I'm in," he declares, his voice filled with conviction. "Count me and my crew in for security. We'll make sure the event goes off without a hitch."

The gang members exchange nods of agreement, their expressions reflecting a mix of determination and pride. They may come from different backgrounds and walks of life, but in this moment, they are united in their commitment to ensuring the success of the concert and the safety of all who attend.

In the midst of their planning for the unity concert, Tupac Shakur and the gang members recognize an opportunity not just to celebrate unity, but to actively empower and uplift their community. Inspired by the vision of Maya Angelou's arts education and Malcolm X's classes on discipline and values, they see the concert as a platform to recruit youth and provide them with opportunities for personal growth and development.

"Tupac, my brother," one of the gang members speaks up, his voice filled with determination, "what if we use this concert to reach out to the youth in our community? We can encourage them to join Maya Angelou's arts education program and Malcolm

X's classes on discipline and values. It's a chance to give them hope, to show them that there's more to life than the streets."

Tupac's eyes light up with excitement as he considers the idea. "That's brilliant," he exclaims, his voice filled with enthusiasm. "We can set up booths at the concert where youth can sign up for these programs. We can even have representatives from Maya and Malcolm's organizations there to talk to them about the benefits of getting involved."

The gang members nod in agreement, their expressions reflecting a mix of determination and pride. They may have come from troubled backgrounds themselves, but they recognize the importance of investing in the next generation, of giving them the tools and resources they need to succeed in life.

As they make plans for the recruitment drive at the concert, Tupac and the gang members feel a sense of purpose and fulfillment wash over them. They know that by reaching out to the youth in their community, by offering them opportunities for education and personal growth, they can make a meaningful difference in their lives—and in the future of their community as a whole. And with Maya Angelou and Malcolm X's guidance and inspiration guiding their efforts, they know that anything is possible.

Bob Marley and Whitney Houston Perform

In a momentous event that transcends boundaries and unites hearts, Bob Marley and Whitney Houston take to the stage for a benefit concert unlike any other. With millions of people from all walks of life in attendance, the city of Orlando becomes a symbol of unity, solidarity, and hope.

As Bob's soulful melodies and Whitney's powerful vocals fill the air, the crowd sways and sings along, their spirits lifted by the music and the message of love and togetherness that permeates the atmosphere. In the midst of the chaos and division that often plague their city, the people of Orlando find a sense of peace and connection as they come together to support a common cause.

But it's not just the music that brings them together—it's the sense of purpose and community that the concert represents. With proceeds going towards initiatives for arts education, discipline, and values, the event becomes a catalyst for positive change, empowering youth and fostering a sense of belonging and hope for the future.

During the concert, Bob Marley wails *"Emancipate yourselves from mental slavery. None but ourselves can free our minds. Have no fear for atomic energy. 'Cause none of them can stop the time."* The people got wild!

As the night wears on and the concert draws to a close, Bob and Whitney stand side by side on stage, their voices blending in harmony as they sing a powerful anthem of unity and resilience. And as the final notes fade away, the crowd erupts into applause, their hearts filled with gratitude and inspiration. Just then Whitney hits angelic notes and sings, *"I want one moment in time. When I'm more than I thought I could be. When all of my dreams are a heart beat away. And the answers are all up to me. Give me one moment in time"* The people break into shouts of joy.

In the days and weeks that follow, the impact of the concert reverberates throughout the city, bringing people together in ways they never thought possible. Neighborhoods once divided by fear and suspicion come together to support one another, and the seeds of hope and possibility that were planted at the concert begin to take root and flourish.

For the people of Orlando, the benefit concert becomes more than just a night of music—it becomes a turning point, a moment of transformation and renewal. And as they look towards the future, they do so with a renewed sense of optimism and determination, knowing that together, they can overcome any challenge and build a brighter tomorrow for themselves and their children.

Maya Angelou's Classes in the Arts become a Huge Success

Following the stirring performances and powerful messages of unity at the benefit concert, hundreds of attendees eagerly sign up for Maya Angelou's arts classes. Drawn by the promise of creativity, self-expression, and personal growth, people from all walks of life flock to join the program, eager to explore their artistic talents and connect with their community in a meaningful way.

Maya emphatically states *"We must infuse our lives with art. Our national leaders must be informed that we want them to use our taxes to support street theatre in order to oppose street gangs. We should have a well-supported regional theatre in order to oppose regionalism."* Maya Angelou's classes quickly become a beacon of light and inspiration in the city of Orlando, attracting students of all ages and backgrounds. From aspiring poets and painters to seasoned artists looking to hone their craft, each participant finds a welcoming and nurturing environment where their creativity can flourish.

Under Maya's guidance, students are encouraged to explore their innermost thoughts and feelings, to express themselves through various artistic mediums, and to connect with one another on a deeper level. Through workshops, performances, and community projects, they discover the transformative power of art to heal, to inspire, and to bring people together.

As word spreads about the success of Maya Angelou's arts classes, the program continues to grow in popularity, drawing even more participants eager to experience the magic of creativity and self-discovery. From local schools and community centers to outreach programs and youth organizations, Maya's classes become an integral part of the fabric of Orlando's cultural landscape, enriching the lives of countless individuals and strengthening the bonds of community and connection.

And as the legacy of Maya Angelou's teachings continues to spread throughout the city, her vision of a world where art serves as a catalyst for positive change and personal transformation becomes a reality. In the hearts and minds of her students, her words echo long after the final brushstroke is painted or the last stanza is recited, inspiring them to embrace their creativity, follow their passions, and make a difference in the world around them. She always told her students *"I believe in living a poetic life, an art full life. Everything we do from the way we raise our children to the way we welcome our friends is part of a large canvas we are creating."*

Malcolm X's Classes on Discipline and Values Fill Up

In the wake of the transformative benefit concert in Orlando, Malcolm X's classes on discipline and core values experience an overwhelming surge in enrollment. Inspired by the message of unity and empowerment from the concert, young people from all walks of life eagerly flock to join the program, seeking guidance and mentorship in their journey towards personal growth and self-improvement.

Malcolm X's classes quickly become a cornerstone of the community, providing a safe and supportive space for youth to learn and grow. Through a combination of lectures, discussions, and practical exercises, students delve into topics such as self-discipline, responsibility, respect, and resilience, gaining valuable insights and skills that they can apply to their everyday lives.

As the weeks go by, the impact of Malcolm X's classes becomes increasingly apparent in the community. Young people who once struggled with discipline and direction begin to show remarkable changes in their behavior and attitude, demonstrating newfound confidence, focus, and determination in their actions.

In the streets of Orlando, stories abound of former troublemakers turning their lives around, of youth finding purpose and direction, and of communities coming together to support one another in their journey towards positive change. Crime rates begin to drop, school attendance rates rise, and a sense of hope and optimism fills the air as people witness the tangible impact of Malcolm X's teachings on their community. He would tell his students *"Education is the passport to the future, for tomorrow belongs to those who prepare for it today."*

But perhaps the most remarkable aspect of Malcolm X's classes is the ripple effect they have on those who participate. As students apply the principles they learn in class to their everyday lives, they become role models and mentors for others in their community, inspiring them to strive for excellence and pursue their dreams with passion and determination.

And as the legacy of Malcolm X's classes continues to spread throughout Orlando, the youth of the city emerge as leaders and agents of change, empowered to shape their own destiny and create a brighter future for themselves and their community. Through discipline, determination, and a commitment to core values, they are prove that positive transformation is not only possible—it's happening right before their eyes.

Tupac Rally's the People to Join His Self Defense Program

In the wake of the powerful unity concert and the surge of inspiration it brought to the community, Tupac Shakur takes to the streets of Orlando to rally the people to join his self-defense program. With his magnetic charisma and passionate conviction, Tupac captures the hearts and minds of the people, drawing them in with his message of empowerment and resilience.

He begins by emphatically stating, *"Why am I fighting to live, If I am just living to fight. Why am I trying to see. When there aint nothing in sight. Why am I trying to give, When no one gives me a try. Why am I dying to live, If I am just living to die?"* As Tupac stands on a makeshift stage, his voice booming with passion and purpose, a crowd begins to gather around him. Young and old, men and women, from all walks of life, they listen intently as Tupac speaks of the importance of self-defense and the need for people to stand up for themselves and their community in the face of adversity.

"Brothers and sisters," Tupac begins, his voice ringing out with clarity and conviction, "we live in a world where violence and oppression are all too common. But we don't have to accept it. We have the power to fight back, to defend ourselves and our loved ones, and to reclaim our dignity and our rights."

The crowd cheers in agreement, their fists raised in solidarity. They are drawn to Tupac's passion and charisma, inspired by his unwavering belief in their ability to make a difference.

"We can't rely on others to protect us," Tupac continues, his voice rising with urgency. "We have to take matters into our own hands. That's why I'm starting this self-defense program—to teach you how to defend yourselves, to empower you to stand up to injustice, and to build a community of strength and resilience."

The people nod in agreement, their eyes shining with determination. They are eager to learn from Tupac, to gain the skills and confidence they need to protect themselves and their community.

As the rally comes to a close, Tupac looks out at the crowd with pride and satisfaction. He knows that he has touched a nerve, awakened a sense of empowerment and solidarity in the people of Orlando. And as they flock to join his self-defense program, he is confident that together, they will stand strong and united in the face of whatever challenges lie ahead.

The Blackstone Alliance Turn Orlando Around

In a remarkable turn of events, the emergence of the Blackstone Alliance: Malcolm X, Bob Marley, Tupac Shakur, Whitney Houston, Martin Luther King Jr., and Maya Angelou ignites a wave of transformation throughout Orlando, Florida. Within just four months, the city undergoes a profound and inspiring metamorphosis, flourishing in business, education, and peace.

Under the guidance of these influential figures, Orlando experiences a renaissance of entrepreneurship and economic growth. Businesses thrive as the community rallies behind initiatives to support local entrepreneurs and foster innovation. With a renewed focus on economic empowerment and opportunity for all, unemployment rates plummet and prosperity spreads throughout the city.

In the realm of education, Maya Angelou's arts classes and Malcolm X's discipline and core values program become cornerstones of the community, empowering youth with the knowledge, skills, and confidence they need to succeed. Schools become hubs of creativity and learning, with students inspired to pursue their passions and achieve their dreams. As a result, graduation rates soar, and a new generation of leaders emerges, poised to shape the future of Orlando and beyond.

But perhaps most significantly, Orlando experiences a newfound sense of peace and unity, as the teachings of Martin Luther King Jr. and the activism of Tupac Shakur inspire people to come together in solidarity and compassion. Crime rates drop, and neighborhoods once plagued by violence and division are transformed into vibrant, thriving communities where people of all backgrounds live and work together in harmony.

As the city basks in the glow of its newfound prosperity and peace, the impact of these visionary leaders reverberates far beyond its borders, inspiring hope and change in communities around the world. Orlando becomes a shining example of what is possible when people come together with a shared vision and a commitment to creating a better world for all. And as the city continues to flourish, its residents stand as living testaments to the power of unity, compassion, and the indomitable human spirit.

Martin Luther King Jr. Sees His Dream Become a Reality

As Martin Luther King Jr. marches through the streets of Orlando, a sea of people gathers around him, their voices raised in joyful celebration. They wave banners and signs emblazoned with messages of hope and equality, their faces radiant with pride and excitement. For many, this moment is the culmination of years of struggle and sacrifice—a testament to the power of Dr. King's dream and the enduring spirit of the civil rights movement.

As Dr. King walks, he is greeted with cheers and applause from the crowd, who hail him and the Blackstone six as heroes and visionaries. They recount the struggles and triumphs of the past, from the marches and protests to the landmark victories in the fight for civil rights. And as they march together through the streets of Orlando, they carry with them the torch of justice and equality, lighting the way for future generations to follow.

Martin Luther emphatically declares to the crowd *"One of the great liabilities of history is that all too many people fail to remain awake through great periods of social change. Every society has its protectors of status quo and its fraternities of the indifferent who are notorious for sleeping through revolutions. Today, our very survival depends on our ability to stay awake, to adjust to new ideas, to remain vigilant and to face the challenge of change."*

For Dr. King, this moment is deeply moving—a validation of his lifelong commitment to justice and equality for all people. As he looks out at the sea of faces before him, he sees the faces of those who have fought alongside him, who have stood up against injustice and oppression, and who have dared to dream of a better world. And as they march together, side by side, he knows that his dream has finally become a reality.

But Dr. King also knows that the work is far from over. Even as they celebrate their victories, there are still challenges ahead—inequality, poverty, and discrimination still plague their society. But with the spirit of unity and determination that fills the streets of Orlando today, Dr. King is confident that they can overcome any obstacle and continue to march forward towards a future of justice, equality, and peace for all.

Orlando Florida Because a Mecca for Black People

In the wake of the Blackstone Alliance's efforts to uplift the black community in Orlando, word spreads like wildfire across the country. The alliance's focus on education, the arts, and discipline, combined with their unyielding commitment to justice and empowerment, captures the imagination of black people from all walks of life. Orlando, once seen as just a theme park city, suddenly becomes a beacon of hope—a promised land for black people seeking a better future.

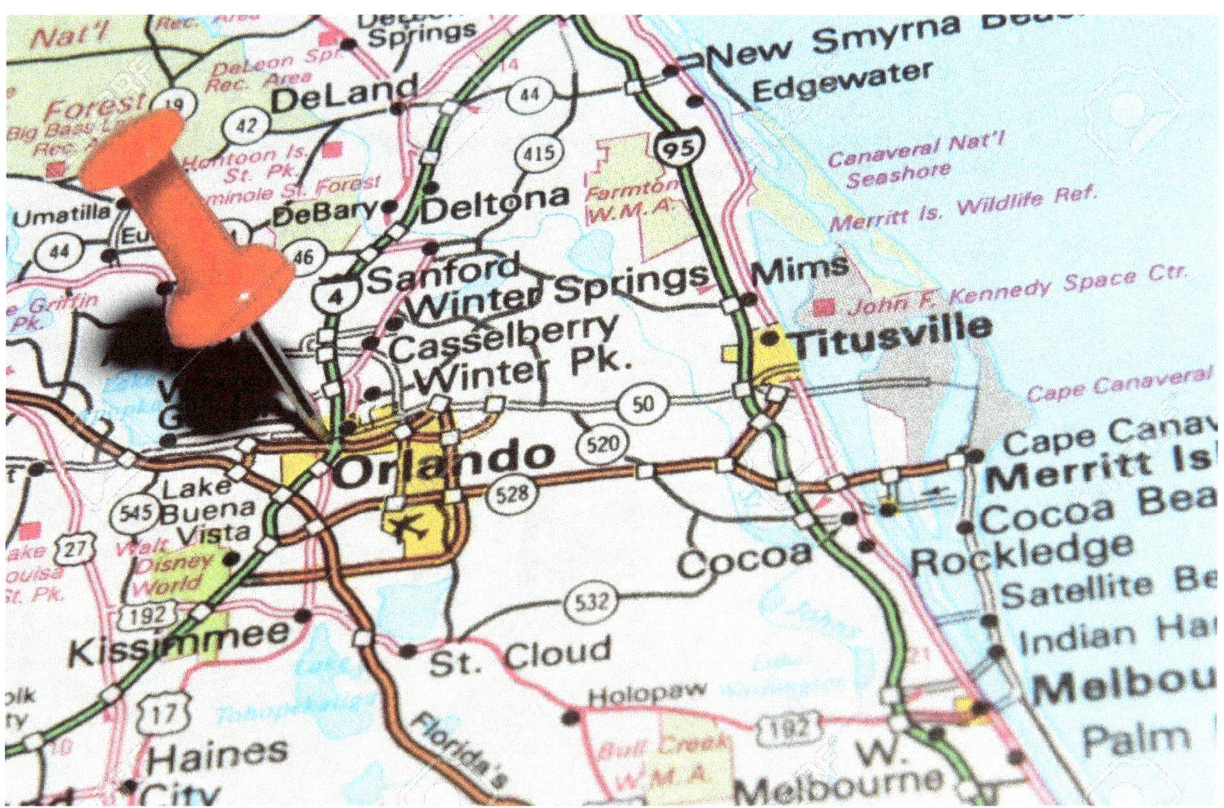

From cities and towns across the nation, black families pack their bags and make the journey to Orlando, drawn by the promise of opportunity and equality. They come seeking refuge from the systemic racism and oppression that has plagued their communities for generations, and they come with a sense of hope and determination that the Blackstone Alliance has instilled in them.

As they arrive in Orlando, they are greeted with open arms by the city's black residents, who welcome them into their communities with warmth and solidarity. Together, they build a vibrant and thriving enclave within the city—a place where black culture and heritage are celebrated, and where the principles of unity and empowerment are lived out every day.

In this new promised land, black people find opportunities for education, employment, and entrepreneurship that were once out of reach. They find a sense of belonging and pride in their identity, and they find allies in the fight for justice and equality. And as they put down roots and make their mark on the city, they contribute to the rich tapestry of arts and culture that defines Orlando.

But perhaps most importantly, they find hope—for themselves, for their children, and for future generations to come. In Orlando, they see the promise of a brighter future—a future where the dreams of freedom, equality, and justice that have long been denied to them can finally become a reality. And as they stand together in solidarity, they know that with the Blackstone Alliance leading the way, anything is possible.

The Peace is Short Lived

Just as Orlando begins to thrive, another tragedy strikes. When news comes out of yet another tragic incident of police violence spreads through the streets of Orlando, the city's fragile peace is shattered once again. The shooting of an unarmed black man by a white police officer ignites a firestorm of anger, frustration, and despair within the black community, reigniting long-standing tensions and grievances.

For many in Orlando, the news is a painful reminder of the systemic racism and injustice that continues to plague their city. Despite the efforts of the Blackstone Alliance and other community leaders to uplift and empower the black community, the specter of police brutality looms large, casting a dark shadow over their hopes and aspirations.

As the details of the shooting emerge, outrage mounts, and calls for justice reverberate through the streets. The Blackstone Alliance, led by Malcolm X, Bob Marley, Maya Angelou, and Martin Luther King Jr, mobilizes their followers, organizing protests, demonstrations, and acts of civil disobedience to demand accountability for the officer responsible.

But amid the anger and frustration, there is also a sense of weariness—a feeling that despite their best efforts, the cycle of violence and injustice continues unabated. For many in Orlando's black community, the shooting serves as a painful reminder of the long road ahead—a road fraught with obstacles and challenges, but also filled with hope and determination.

As tensions escalate and the city braces for unrest, the question remains: will Orlando rise to the challenge and confront the systemic racism and injustice that plagues its streets? Or will the city's hopes for peace and equality once again be dashed against the rocks of indifference and apathy? One thing is clear: the struggle for justice and equality in Orlando is far from over.

Orlando Turns into a War Zone

As tensions in Orlando reach a boiling point following the tragic shooting of an unarmed black man by a white police officer, the city descends into chaos and violence. What begins as peaceful protests and demonstrations quickly escalates into all-out conflict, as anger and frustration give way to riots, looting, and destruction.

In the streets of Orlando, clashes erupt between protesters and law enforcement, with tear gas and rubber bullets filling the air as both sides dig in their heels. Buildings are set ablaze, storefronts are smashed, and chaos reigns supreme as the city is consumed by the flames of unrest.

Amidst the turmoil, innocent bystanders are caught in the crossfire, their lives hanging in the balance as the city teeters on the brink of collapse. The sounds of sirens and gunfire echo through the streets, as emergency responders struggle to maintain order in the face of overwhelming chaos.

In the midst of the violence, the Blackstone Alliance works tirelessly to quell the unrest and restore peace to the city. Led by figures like Whitney Houston and Martin Luther King Jr, they call for calm and unity, urging their followers to channel their anger into constructive action and to reject violence and destruction as a means of achieving justice.

But their efforts are met with resistance, as deep-seated anger and frustration boil over into acts of violence and retribution. The city becomes a battleground, with no end in sight to the bloodshed and destruction that ravages its streets.

As the sun sets on Orlando, the city lies smoldering and broken, its once-vibrant streets now wounded by the scars of conflict and despair. The promise of peace and prosperity that once seemed within reach has been shattered, replaced by a sense of fear and uncertainty that hangs heavy in the air.

Tupac Mobilizes His Forces

In the midst of the chaos and violence engulfing Orlando, Tupac Shakur emerges as a beacon of hope and leadership, organizing a diverse coalition of individuals from all walks of life to fight against police corruption and injustice. Drawing on his charisma, influence, and unwavering commitment to social justice, Tupac rallies gang members, community activists, and even sympathetic police officers to his cause, uniting them in a common struggle against the systemic oppression and abuse of power that plagues their city.

With Tupac's guidance and leadership, the unlikely alliance sets out to expose and root out corruption within the police force, shining a light on the abuses of power and the culture of impunity that have allowed injustice to flourish for far too long. Together, they work tirelessly to hold corrupt officers and officials accountable for their actions, demanding transparency, accountability, and reform within the criminal justice system.

Tupac declares *"We are being wiped off the face of this earth. At an extremely alarming rate. And even more alarming is the fact that we are not fighting back."* But their fight is not without its challenges. As they confront entrenched interests and powerful adversaries, they face threats, intimidation, and violence from those who seek to maintain the status quo. But Tupac and his allies refuse to back down, drawing strength from their shared commitment to justice and equality, and their belief in the transformative power of collective action.

As the battle against police corruption rages on, Tupac's leadership inspires others to join the fight, galvanizing a groundswell of support and solidarity from across the city. Together, they become a force to be reckoned with, challenging the forces of injustice and oppression at every turn and laying the groundwork for a brighter, more just future for Orlando and its residents.

Orlando Mayor Declares a State of Emergency

In response to the escalating unrest and violence plaguing Orlando, the city government makes the decision to declare a state of emergency and implement martial law. This drastic measure is taken in an effort to restore order, protect public safety, and prevent further damage to property and loss of life.

Under martial law, the city government assumes expanded authority and control over the city, allowing for the deployment of additional law enforcement and military personnel to enforce order. Curfews are imposed, public gatherings are restricted, and individuals become subject to increased surveillance and scrutiny in order to quell the unrest and restore government control.

The people of Orlando now see their civil liberties gone and an increase in the abuse of power. The city government is keenly aware of these concerns and pledges to uphold the rights and freedoms of all residents, even as they take drastic steps to restore order. The black community has now lost all trust in the Orlando city government.

Many people play Bob Marley's lyrics *"Get up, stand up, stand up for your right. Get up, stand up, stand up for your right. Don't give up the fight."*

Tupac's Forces Fight the National Guard

As the city of Orlando descends into chaos and martial law is declared, Tupac's alliance finds itself in direct conflict with both the police and the National Guard. Determined to fight against what they perceive as injustice and oppression, they stand firm in their resolve to resist the authorities and defend the rights of the people.

Tupac's alliance, composed of gang members, community activists, and sympathetic police officers, mobilizes their forces and takes to the streets, facing off against the heavily armed and well-trained police and military personnel. With makeshift weapons and makeshift barricades, they engage in fierce skirmishes and clashes, refusing to back down in the face of overwhelming force.

Despite the odds stacked against them, Tupac's alliance fights with courage and determination, driven by a deep-seated belief in their cause and a commitment to justice and equality. They are fueled by the memory of those who have been unjustly killed and the desire to ensure that their deaths are not in vain.

As the battles rage on, the streets of Orlando become a battleground, with tear gas, gunfire, and explosions echoing through the night. The air is thick with smoke and the scent of fear, as both sides dig in their heels and refuse to give ground.

But amidst the chaos and violence, there are moments of solidarity and unity, as people from all walks of life come together to support Tupac's alliance and resist the authorities. They stand shoulder to shoulder, united in their determination to fight for a better future, even in the face of seemingly insurmountable odds.

As the conflict escalates, the stakes become higher, and the outcome becomes increasingly uncertain. But for Tupac's alliance, the fight is not just about winning—it's about standing up for what they believe in, even in the face of overwhelming adversity. And as they continue to battle against the forces of oppression and injustice, they know that their struggle is far from over. Tupac shouts, *"Never surrender, it's all about the faith you got: don't ever stop, just push it 'till you hit the top and if you drop, at least you know you gave your all to be true to you, that way you can never fall."*

Tupac's Forces Win the Battle of I-Drive

In a dramatic turn of events, Tupac's alliance achieves a significant victory in the heart of Orlando as they successfully repel the police and National Guard forces in the battle of I-Drive. The streets are strewn with barricades and debris as the two sides clash in a fierce and intense confrontation, but against all odds, Tupac's alliance emerges triumphant.

With their backs against the wall and their resolve tested to the limit, Tupac's alliance fights with courage and determination, refusing to yield in the face of overwhelming force. They stand firm against the onslaught of tear gas and rubber bullets, rallying together in a display of solidarity and defiance that inspires all who witness it.

As the battle rages on, the tide begins to turn in favor of Tupac's alliance, as they gain ground and push the police forces back. With each passing moment, their confidence grows, fueled by the knowledge that they are fighting for a just cause and that victory is within their grasp.

And then, in a moment of triumph and vindication, the police forces begin to retreat, their ranks broken and their resolve shaken by the ferocity of Tupac's alliance. The streets of I-Drive erupt in jubilation as the people celebrate their hard-fought victory, their cheers echoing through the night as a symbol of hope and defiance. Tupac shouts to the crowd, *"Trust me I never lose. Either I win or learn from it".*

But even as they celebrate their success, Tupac's alliance knows that the fight is far from over. The battle of I-Drive may have been won, but the struggle against injustice and oppression continues. With their spirits renewed and their determination unbroken, they stand ready to face whatever challenges lie ahead, confident in their ability to bring about real change and build a better future for all of Orlando's residents.

Orlando City Council and Police are Furious

As news of Tupac's alliance's victory in the battle of I-Drive spreads, panic and frustration grip the Orlando city government as they come to terms with the reality that they are losing control of the situation. The realization that they may have to evacuate the city sends shockwaves through the ranks of city officials, who are faced with the daunting task of addressing the escalating crisis.

Furious and desperate, city officials scramble to regain control and quell the growing unrest, but their efforts are hampered by the sheer magnitude of the situation and the determination of Tupac's alliance to resist their authority. As tensions continue to escalate and violence spreads throughout the city, the prospect of evacuation becomes increasingly likely, forcing city officials to confront the harsh reality of their inability to maintain order and protect their own safety.

In the face of mounting pressure and uncertainty, the city government grapples with the difficult decision of whether to evacuate Orlando and abandon their responsibilities to its residents. The prospect of such a drastic measure weighs heavily on their minds, as they weigh the potential consequences of leaving the city in the hands of those who have risen up against them.

But as they debate their next course of action, one thing becomes clear: the situation in Orlando has reached a critical juncture, and decisive measures must be taken to address the underlying issues of injustice and inequality that have fueled the unrest. Whether the city government can rise to the challenge and confront these issues head-on remains to be seen, but one thing is certain: the fate of Orlando hangs in the balance, and the decisions made in the coming days will shape its future for years to come.

Tupac is Crowned King of Orlando

In a stunning turn of events, Tupac's alliance achieves another decisive victory in the heart of Orlando as they successfully seize control of City Hall, forcing the mayor to flee in the face of their overwhelming strength and determination. With the city government in disarray and their authority effectively dismantled, Tupac emerges as the de facto leader of Orlando, hailed by his supporters as the new King of Orlando.

The battle of City Hall is a testament to the power of grassroots activism and collective action, as Tupac's alliance—comprised of gang members, community activists, and sympathetic police officers—rallies together to challenge the entrenched forces of oppression and corruption that have long held sway over the city. With their victory, they send a clear message to the powers that be: the people of Orlando will no longer tolerate injustice and inequality, and they will fight tirelessly to reclaim their city and build a better future for all its residents.

As Tupac assumes his new role as King of Orlando, he pledges to lead with integrity, compassion, and a steadfast commitment to justice and equality. With the support of his allies and the unwavering loyalty of the people, he sets out to implement sweeping reforms aimed at addressing the root causes of the city's problems and creating a more just and equitable society for all.

But Tupac knows that the road ahead will not be easy. The challenges facing Orlando are many, and the forces of oppression and injustice are deeply entrenched. Yet he is undeterred, knowing that with the strength of his conviction and the support of his people, anything is possible.

As he stands atop the steps of City Hall, surveying the city that he now leads, Tupac is filled with a sense of hope and determination. For the first time in a long time, the future of Orlando looks bright, and the people are ready to follow their new King into a new era of peace, prosperity, and justice for all. Tupac declares, *"You know nothing can stop me but loss of breath, and I'm still breathing so it's still on. I'm not saying I'm gonna change the world, but I guarantee that I will spark the brain that will change the world."*

The People of Orlando Pledge Loyalty to Tupac

With Tupac's alliance emerging victorious and Tupac himself being hailed as the King of Orlando, the people of the city rally around their new leader with unwavering loyalty and support. Inspired by his courage, charisma, and commitment to justice, they pledge their allegiance to Tupac and his vision for a better future for Orlando.

From every corner of the city, residents come forward to express their solidarity with Tupac and his cause, eager to join him in the fight against injustice and oppression. They see in him a beacon of hope and a symbol of change, and they are determined to stand by his side as he leads them into a new era of peace and prosperity.

Amidst the chaos and uncertainty of the times, Tupac's leadership offers a sense of stability and direction, providing the people of Orlando with hope for a brighter future. They believe in his ability to bring about real change and to address the deep-seated issues that have plagued their city for far too long.

With their loyalty and support, Tupac's alliance grows stronger by the day, as more and more people join the movement to reclaim their city and build a more just and equitable society. Together, they stand united in their determination to create a better future for themselves and for generations to come.

As Tupac looks out upon the sea of faces that have gathered to pledge their loyalty to him, he is filled with a profound sense of gratitude and humility. He knows that the road ahead will be long and difficult, but with the support of the people of Orlando behind him, he is confident that they will succeed in their quest for justice and equality. And as they embark on this journey together, they do so with a renewed sense of purpose and hope, ready to confront whatever challenges may lie ahead and to build a brighter future for all.

Tupac Meets with Blackstone Alliance

With the people of Orlando rallying behind him and pledging their loyalty, Tupac wastes no time in assembling his closest allies to plan for the city's future. Recognizing the need for unity and collaboration, he calls a meeting with the leaders of the Blackstone Alliance, including influential figures Malcolm X and Maya Angelou, to chart a course forward for Orlando.

Gathered together in a secluded location, Tupac and the members of Blackstone engage in a frank and impassioned discussion about the challenges facing their city and the steps that must be taken to overcome them. They exchange ideas, share insights, and debate strategies, drawing on their collective wisdom and experience to craft a vision for a better Orlando.

At the heart of their discussions is a commitment to justice, equality, and empowerment for all of Orlando's residents, regardless of race, gender, or background. They envision a city where every person has access to quality education, economic opportunity, and a voice in the decisions that affect their lives.

But they also recognize that achieving this vision will require hard work, dedication, and sacrifice. They know that the road ahead will be long and difficult, and that they will face many obstacles and challenges along the way. But they are undeterred, knowing that with unity, determination, and a shared sense of purpose, anything is possible.

As the meeting draws to a close, Tupac and the members of Blackstone emerge with a renewed sense of purpose and resolve. They know that the task ahead will not be easy, but they are committed to working together to build a brighter future for Orlando and all who call it home. With their vision set and their determination strong, they are ready to embark on this journey together, confident in their ability to overcome whatever challenges may come their way and to create a city that truly lives up to its promise of equality, justice, and opportunity for all.

Whitney Houston Apologizes to Tupac

After the meeting with Tupac and the Blackstone Alliance comes to a close, Whitney Houston approaches Tupac with a sense of humility and sincerity. With a deep sense of regret weighing on her heart, she offers him a heartfelt apology for ever doubting his methods and intentions.

In a voice filled with emotion, Whitney expresses her remorse for questioning Tupac's approach to bringing about change in Orlando. She acknowledges that her skepticism was born out of fear and uncertainty, but she now sees the wisdom and courage in his actions.

With tears in her eyes, Whitney vows her unwavering support to Tupac and his vision for Orlando. She pledges to stand by his side through thick and thin, to lend her voice and influence to the cause, and to do whatever it takes to help realize their shared dream of a better future for the city.

Tupac, moved by Whitney's sincerity and humility, accepts her apology with grace and gratitude. He embraces her as a valued ally and friend, knowing that her support will be instrumental in the journey ahead. Together, they stand united in their commitment to building a more just, equitable, and compassionate Orlando for all its residents.

Blackstone Alliance Move into the Castle

In a symbolic gesture that captures the spirit of unity and renewal sweeping through Orlando, the Theme Park's Castle is declared the new capital building of the city. As the iconic symbol of magic and dreams, the castle embodies the hopes and aspirations of the people of Orlando as they embark on a new chapter in their history.

With its majestic towers and grand halls, the Castle becomes the new headquarters for the Blackstone Alliance, serving as a beacon of hope and inspiration for all who seek justice, equality, and empowerment. From its storied halls, Tupac and his allies will work tirelessly to build a brighter future for Orlando, drawing strength from the legacy of resilience and determination that the castle represents.

As the news spreads throughout the city, there is a palpable sense of excitement and anticipation in the air. For many, the castle represents a fresh start and a new beginning, a symbol of the city's resilience and determination to overcome adversity and build a better future for all.

In the days and weeks that follow, the Castle becomes a hub of activity and innovation, as the Blackstone Alliance sets to work implementing their vision for Orlando. From its halls, they will plan and strategize, forge alliances and build coalitions, and lay the groundwork for a more just, equitable, and inclusive city for all its residents.

As the sun sets on the horizon, casting a golden glow over the castle's towers, the people of Orlando look to the future with hope and optimism. And as they stand in the shadow of the Castle, they know that together, they can overcome any challenge and achieve their dreams of a better tomorrow.

Tupac Announces the new Government

In a historic announcement that marks a new era for Orlando, Tupac stands before the people of the city to unveil his new government and cabinet members. With a sense of pride and determination, he introduces the leaders who will help him shape the future of Orlando and lead the city into a new era of peace, prosperity, and justice for all.

First and foremost, Tupac declares that Malcolm X will serve as his chief advisor, drawing on his wisdom, experience, and unwavering commitment to justice to guide the government's decisions and policies. As a champion of civil rights and equality, Malcolm X's leadership will be instrumental in shaping the direction of the city and ensuring that the voices of the marginalized and oppressed are heard and respected.

Next, Tupac announces that Maya Angelou will take on the role of overseeing the city's education system as head of the Board of Education. With her passion for learning and dedication to empowering young minds, Maya Angelou will work tirelessly to ensure that every child in Orlando has access to a quality education and the opportunity to succeed.

Whitney Houston is named as the head of the City Arts Department, tasked with promoting creativity, expression, and cultural enrichment throughout Orlando. With her talent and passion for the arts, Whitney will oversee initiatives to support local artists, musicians, and performers, and to bring the magic of the arts to every corner of the city.

Bob Marley is appointed to lead the Foreign Affairs Department, leveraging his global influence and diplomatic skills to strengthen Orlando's connections with the world and promote peace and cooperation on the international stage. Through diplomacy and dialogue, Bob Marley will work to build bridges between Orlando and the global community, fostering understanding and mutual respect between peoples and nations.

Finally, Tupac announces that Martin Luther King Jr. will serve as the head of the Church, overseeing spiritual and moral guidance for the people of Orlando. With his message of love, compassion, and unity, Martin Luther King Jr. will inspire the city to come together as one community, bound by a shared commitment to justice, equality, and humanity.

As Tupac introduces his new government and cabinet members, the people of Orlando erupt into cheers and applause, filled with hope and optimism for the future. With their leadership and guidance, Tupac's alliance will work tirelessly to build a city that lives up to its promise of equality, justice, and opportunity for all. And as they embark on this journey together, they do so with a sense of purpose and determination, knowing that with unity and determination, anything is possible.

Orlando Renamed the Kingdom of Zion, Expands it's Territory

In a momentous meeting of the Blackstone Alliance, Tupac and his advisors gather to discuss the future of their movement and the city of Orlando. As they deliberate on how best to solidify their vision of a just and equitable society, they come to a bold and transformative decision: to rename Orlando the 'Kingdom of Zion'.

This symbolic gesture represents a break from the past and a reimagining of the city as a beacon of hope and progress for all who inhabit it. By adopting the name Kingdom of

Zion, they affirm their commitment to building a community founded on principles of justice, equality, and empowerment.

But the transformation doesn't stop there. In a bold move to expand their influence and reach, the Blackstone Alliance decides to extend their territory to cover the entire Central Florida area, including cities like Tampa, Kissimmee, and Daytona Beach. This strategic expansion gives them access to both the Atlantic coast and the Gulf of Mexico, opening up new opportunities for trade, commerce, and cultural exchange.

As the news of these decisions spreads throughout the region, there is a sense of excitement and anticipation among the people of Central Florida. They see in the Kingdom of Zion a vision of a better future, where unity, compassion, and justice prevail.

With their expanded territory and renewed sense of purpose, Tupac and the Blackstone Alliance are poised to lead their people into a new era of prosperity and progress. Together, they will build a kingdom where all are welcome, and where the dreams of a better tomorrow can become a reality for generations to come.

Tupac Meets with Martin Luther King Jr

In a solemn meeting between Tupac and Martin Luther King Jr., the weighty concerns of moral integrity and societal corruption take center stage. As they engage in earnest dialogue, King expresses his deep-seated concerns about the moral fiber of the people within the Kingdom of Zion. With a heavy heart, he confides in Tupac, cautioning him about the pervasive presence of corruption within the minds and hearts of many individuals.

King's words carry a profound weight, as he reflects on the inherent fragility of human nature and the potential consequences of moral decay within society. He warns Tupac of the dangers posed by greed, selfishness, and moral complacency, emphasizing the importance of upholding ethical principles and moral values in order to safeguard the integrity and stability of the Kingdom of Zion.

Tupac listens intently to King's words, recognizing the gravity of the situation and the imperative need for vigilance in the face of moral challenges. He acknowledges the inherent complexity of human nature and the constant struggle between light and darkness within each individual. With humility and appreciation, Tupac accepts King's counsel, pledging to remain vigilant and steadfast in his commitment to upholding the moral principles and values that underpin the Kingdom of Zion.

As they part ways, Tupac carries with him the weight of King's words, reflecting on the profound responsibility of leadership and the imperative need to foster a culture of integrity, compassion, and justice within the Kingdom of Zion. With King's wisdom as his guide, Tupac is determined to confront the challenges of moral decay head-on, ensuring that the Kingdom of Zion remains a beacon of light and hope for all who inhabit it.

Ambassador Bob Marley Goes Across Seas

Bob Marley's diplomatic mission to strengthen trade relations with the Kingdom of Zion takes him on a journey across continents, where he visits nations eager to engage in commerce and partnership. His first stop is in Ghana, where he is warmly welcomed by government officials and business leaders eager to explore opportunities for trade and collaboration. In Kenya, Ethiopia, Brazil, and Colombia, similar receptions await Bob Marley and his delegation, as leaders from each nation express their enthusiasm for forging closer ties with the Kingdom of Zion.

In Ghana, Bob Marley is greeted with the sounds of traditional music and the sight of vibrant colors as he meets with government officials and business leaders to discuss potential trade agreements. The rich cultural heritage and burgeoning economy of Ghana offer promising opportunities for partnership, and Bob Marley is eager to explore avenues for collaboration that will benefit both nations.

In Kenya and Ethiopia, Bob Marley is humbled by the warm hospitality and profound sense of unity and pride he encounters among the people. As he discusses trade opportunities with government officials and entrepreneurs, he is struck by the potential for economic growth and development that exists within these nations, and he is committed to fostering mutually beneficial relationships that will contribute to their prosperity.

In Brazil, Bob Marley is captivated by the vibrant energy and diversity of culture that permeates the streets of Rio de Janeiro and São Paulo. As he meets with government representatives and business leaders, he is inspired by their shared vision for the future and their eagerness to collaborate with the Kingdom of Zion on trade initiatives that will enhance economic opportunities and promote sustainable development.

Finally, in Colombia, Bob Marley is moved by the resilience and determination of the people as they work to overcome challenges and build a brighter future for themselves and their communities. As he engages in discussions with government officials and industry leaders, he is impressed by their commitment to innovation and entrepreneurship, and he sees immense potential for partnership with the Kingdom of Zion that will benefit both nations.

As Bob Marley returns from his diplomatic mission, he does so with a renewed sense of optimism and determination. The warm reception and enthusiastic response he received from leaders across the globe are a testament to the Kingdom of Zion's growing influence and stature on the world stage, and he is confident that the partnerships forged during his journey will pave the way for a future of prosperity and cooperation for all involved.

Martin Luther King Jr. Ends Homelessness

Under the compassionate leadership of Martin Luther King Jr., the Kingdom of Zion embarks on an ambitious initiative to address homelessness and ensure that all its residents have access to food and shelter. With a sense of urgency and determination, King launches programs aimed at providing support and assistance to the most vulnerable members of society. King would walk the streets telling everyone *"Why should there be hunger and deprivation in any land, in any city, at any table, when man has the resources and the scientific know-how to provide all mankind with the basic necessities of life? There is no deficit in human resources. The deficit is in human will. I have the audacity to believe that peoples everywhere can have three meals a day for their bodies, education and culture for their minds, and dignity, equality and freedom for their spirits."*

Through a combination of government resources, community partnerships, and grassroots activism, King's programs quickly gain momentum, offering a lifeline to those in need and helping to lift them out of poverty and despair. Food distribution centers are established, providing nutritious meals to those who are hungry, while shelters are opened to provide safe and secure housing for those who are homeless.

As the programs gain traction and support from across the Kingdom of Zion, the impact is profound and far-reaching. Within just four months, the scourge of homelessness is eradicated, and every resident of the Kingdom has a roof over their head and food on their table. No longer do people have to sleep on the streets or go hungry, as resources are shared equitably and compassionately among all.

The success of King's programs serves as a testament to the power of collective action and the transformative potential of compassionate leadership. By prioritizing the needs of the most vulnerable members of society and mobilizing resources to address systemic injustices, King and the Kingdom of Zion demonstrate their commitment to building a more just, equitable, and compassionate society for all.

As the last homeless person finds shelter and security within the Kingdom of Zion, a sense of pride and accomplishment washes over the community. Together, they have achieved something remarkable, proving that with empathy, determination, and collective action, anything is possible. And as they look to the future, they do so with hope and optimism, knowing that they have the power to overcome any challenge and build a better world for generations to come.

Maya Angelou Develops Educational Excellence

Under the visionary leadership of Maya Angelou, the educational department of the Kingdom of Zion undergoes a transformative evolution, embracing a holistic approach to education that empowers individuals to thrive in all aspects of their lives. With a deep commitment to lifelong learning and personal development, Angelou introduces a comprehensive curriculum that encompasses a wide range of subjects essential for success and well-being.

At the heart of the educational department's new approach is a focus on financial literacy, equipping residents of the Kingdom of Zion with the knowledge and skills they need to make informed decisions about money and manage their finances effectively. Through workshops, seminars, and hands-on activities, individuals learn how to budget, save, invest, and plan for their financial future, laying the foundation for long-term economic stability and prosperity.

In addition to financial literacy, the educational department also places a strong emphasis on health and wellness, recognizing the importance of physical, mental, and emotional well-being in achieving overall success and happiness. Residents are encouraged to prioritize self-care and adopt healthy habits that promote vitality and resilience, with a variety of programs and resources available to support their journey to optimal health.

As part of the educational department's commitment to celebrating and preserving cultural heritage, Angelou introduces courses in black history, ensuring that residents of the Kingdom of Zion have a deep understanding and appreciation of their rich and diverse heritage. Through the study of key historical events, figures, and movements, individuals gain a sense of pride and identity, strengthening their connection to their roots and inspiring them to make meaningful contributions to society.

Entrepreneurship is also a key focus of the educational department, with Angelou recognizing the importance of fostering innovation and creativity in the pursuit of economic empowerment. Residents are encouraged to explore their entrepreneurial spirit and pursue their passions, with support and guidance available to help them turn their ideas into successful businesses and ventures.

Family development is another area of emphasis, with Angelou recognizing the importance of strong, supportive relationships in fostering personal growth and well-being. Through workshops, counseling services, and community events, individuals learn how to cultivate healthy and thriving relationships with their loved ones, creating a foundation of love, trust, and mutual respect that enriches their lives.

Finally, the educational department of the Kingdom of Zion also prioritizes trades education, recognizing the value of practical skills and hands-on experience in preparing individuals for success in the workforce. Through apprenticeships, vocational training programs, and experiential learning opportunities, residents have the opportunity to develop valuable skills in areas such as carpentry, plumbing, electrical work, and more, providing them with pathways to meaningful and fulfilling careers.

As Maya Angelou's vision for the educational department comes to fruition, the residents of the Kingdom of Zion are empowered to pursue their dreams, overcome obstacles, and achieve their full potential. With a holistic approach to education that addresses the needs of the whole person, the Kingdom of Zion becomes a place where individuals thrive, families flourish, and communities prosper, embodying the principles of lifelong learning, personal growth, and empowerment for all.

She finishes her presentation by stating, *"Out of the huts of history's shame, I rise. Up from a past that's rooted in pain, I rise. I'm a black ocean, leaping and wide, Welling and swelling I bear in the tide. Leaving behind nights of terror and fear. I rise. Into a daybreak that's wondrously clear. I rise. Bringing the gifts that my ancestors gave, I am the dream and the hope of the slave. I rise, I rise, I rise."* The people all stood up and broke into a rousing applause.

Whitney Houston's Arts Program Flourishes

Under the inspiring leadership of Whitney Houston, the arts program of the Kingdom of Zion flourishes, becoming a vibrant hub of creativity, expression, and community engagement. With a deep passion for the arts and a commitment to nurturing talent and creativity in the next generation, Houston introduces a wide range of programs and initiatives aimed at empowering children and youth to explore their artistic passions and unleash their creative potential.

Through a diverse array of classes, workshops, and performances, children are provided with opportunities to develop their skills and express themselves through various artistic mediums, including music, dance, theater, visual arts, and more. Whether they're learning to play a musical instrument, honing their acting skills on stage, or creating masterpieces with paint and canvas, children are encouraged to embrace their unique talents and explore their creativity in a supportive and nurturing environment.

Whitney would tell all the parents in her program *"I believe the children are our future. Teach them well and let them lead the way. Show them all the beauty they possess inside. Give them a sense of pride to make it easier. Let the children's laughter remind us how we used to be."*

As children immerse themselves in the arts, they discover new ways to express themselves, build self-confidence, and develop important life skills such as teamwork, communication, and problem-solving. They learn to collaborate with their peers, take risks, and push the boundaries of their creativity, gaining a sense of pride and accomplishment as they see their talents grow and develop.

One of the most significant impacts of Whitney Houston's arts program is its role in reducing juvenile delinquency within the Kingdom of Zion. By providing children with positive outlets for self-expression and personal growth, the arts program offers an alternative to negative influences and destructive behaviors. Children who might otherwise be at risk of getting involved in crime or gangs find a sense of belonging and purpose in the arts, channeling their energy and creativity into productive and meaningful pursuits.

As children become more deeply engaged in the arts, they develop a sense of pride in their accomplishments and a greater appreciation for the value of creativity and self-expression. They discover new passions, forge lasting friendships, and gain a sense of belonging to a community that celebrates their talents and supports their dreams.

Through Whitney Houston's visionary leadership, the arts program of the Kingdom of Zion becomes a shining example of the transformative power of the arts to inspire, uplift, and empower individuals of all ages. As children harness their creativity and explore their passions, they become agents of positive change within their communities, leaving behind a legacy of artistic excellence and cultural enrichment that will endure for generations to come.

The Kingdom of Zion Flourishes in its First Year of Existence

In its inaugural year, the Kingdom of Zion stands as a beacon of hope, prosperity, and unity, achieving remarkable progress and transformation under the visionary leadership of its founders. With trade routes opened and flourishing partnerships established with nations around the world, the Kingdom experiences unprecedented economic growth and prosperity, laying the foundation for a thriving and prosperous future.

The implementation of comprehensive programs in arts and education has a profound impact on the lives of the Kingdom's residents, empowering them to unlock their full potential and pursue their dreams. Through initiatives spearheaded by leaders such as Whitney Houston and Maya Angelou, children and youth are provided with opportunities to explore their creativity, develop their talents, and receive a quality education that equips them with the skills and knowledge they need to succeed in life.

As a result of these efforts, the Kingdom experiences a cultural renaissance, with artistic expression flourishing and creativity blossoming in every corner of society. From vibrant street performances to world-class exhibitions, the arts become a central part of the Kingdom's identity, enriching the lives of its residents and fostering a sense of community and belonging.

But perhaps most importantly, the Kingdom of Zion achieves a monumental milestone in its mission to create a more just and equitable society: the eradication of homelessness. Through the compassionate leadership of Martin Luther King Jr. and the implementation of innovative programs and policies, every resident of the Kingdom now has access to food, shelter, and support, ensuring that no one is left behind or forgotten.

As the people of the Kingdom of Zion reflect on their accomplishments in their first year, they do so with a profound sense of gratitude, pride, and optimism for the future. They have overcome challenges, forged new partnerships, and laid the groundwork for a brighter tomorrow for themselves and future generations to come. And as they look ahead to the years to come, they do so with confidence, knowing that with unity, compassion, and determination, anything is possible in the Kingdom of Zion.

The Kingdom of Zion Faces Challenges in Year Two

As the Kingdom of Zion enters its second year, cracks begin to appear in the facade of unity and prosperity that characterized its early days. Despite the initial successes and achievements, underlying issues of morality and personal conduct begin to surface, casting a shadow over the kingdom's progress and stability.

The warnings of Martin Luther King Jr. about the importance of moral integrity and ethical behavior prove prescient, as many residents of the Kingdom struggle with issues of low self-esteem, moral judgment, and personal responsibility. Instances of fornication, lying, and stealing become increasingly common, eroding the trust and cohesion that once bound the community together.

Moreover, a sense of complacency and entitlement begins to take hold among some members of the population, leading to a culture of laziness and selfishness that undermines the kingdom's collective well-being. Instead of working together for the common good, individuals prioritize their own needs and desires at the expense of others, fueling resentment and conflict within the community.

As tensions simmer and discontent grows, the Kingdom of Zion finds itself at a crossroads, grappling with the difficult task of maintaining its ideals and values in the face of moral decay and social unrest. Leaders and residents alike are forced to confront uncomfortable truths about the state of their society and the challenges that lie ahead.

In response to these challenges, the leaders of the Kingdom must redouble their efforts to promote ethical behavior and personal accountability, recommitting themselves to the principles of justice, compassion, and unity that guided their founding. Through education, outreach, and community engagement, they seek to address the root causes of moral decline and inspire a renewed sense of purpose and responsibility among the people.

As the Kingdom of Zion confronts its internal struggles and strives to overcome the obstacles in its path, it is reminded of the importance of vigilance, resilience, and moral integrity in building a society that truly embodies the values of justice, equality, and righteousness. And though the road ahead may be challenging, the leaders of the Kingdom remain steadfast in their commitment to creating a better future for themselves and their descendants, guided by the timeless principles of truth, love, and compassion.

Tupac Gets Threatened

As tensions rise within the Kingdom of Zion, a new challenge emerges in the form of disgruntled former gang leaders who question Tupac's leadership and threaten to destabilize the kingdom if their demands are not met. These individuals, once powerful figures in the underworld, now seek to assert their influence and regain control over the direction of the kingdom, using intimidation and coercion to advance their agenda.

At the heart of their discontent lies a sense of dissatisfaction with Tupac's leadership style and decision-making process. They feel marginalized and overlooked, believing that their perspectives and concerns are not being adequately addressed or considered by the kingdom's leadership. Frustrated by what they perceive as a lack of representation and inclusion, they begin to agitate for change, demanding a greater voice in the governance of the kingdom and threatening to take drastic action if their demands are not met.

Tupac is faced with a difficult dilemma, torn between the need to maintain order and stability within the kingdom and the desire to address the legitimate grievances of these former gang leaders. On one hand, he recognizes the importance of listening to the concerns of all residents and ensuring that their voices are heard in the decision-making process. On the other hand, he cannot afford to compromise the safety and security of the kingdom or allow it to be held hostage by the threats of a few individuals.

As tensions escalate and the situation becomes increasingly volatile, Tupac must navigate a delicate balancing act, seeking to defuse the situation through dialogue and negotiation while also standing firm in his commitment to upholding the principles of justice, equality, and integrity. With the support of his allies and the backing of the community, he confronts the challenge head-on, refusing to be swayed by threats or intimidation and reaffirming his authority as the rightful leader of the Kingdom of Zion.

The Problems Continue

As challenges persist within the Kingdom of Zion, concerns about family conflict, ongoing drug use, and a breakdown in trust between men and women threaten to undermine the community's unity and cohesion. Despite efforts to address these issues, divisions persist, and discontent simmers beneath the surface, leading some to question the direction of the kingdom and even long for the perceived stability of the past.

Maya Angelou and Martin Luther King Jr., recognizing the urgency of the situation, embark on a series of outreach efforts to engage with the people of Zion directly, offering counsel, guidance, and support to families in need. With compassion and empathy, they listen to the concerns of residents and seek to understand the root causes of their discontent, working tirelessly to bridge divides and promote reconciliation within the community. Martin would continually say, *"We must learn to live together as brothers or perish together as fools."*

Through their outreach efforts, Angelou and King emphasize the importance of communication, empathy, and mutual respect in fostering healthy relationships and resolving conflicts. They encourage families to come together in dialogue, to listen to one another with open hearts and minds, and to seek common ground in the pursuit of peace and understanding.

At the same time, Angelou and King address the issue of drug use within the community, recognizing the devastating impact it can have on individuals and families alike. They advocate for increased access to addiction treatment and support services, as well as initiatives to address the root causes of substance abuse and provide alternative pathways to healing and recovery.

In their efforts to rebuild trust between men and women, Angelou and King emphasize the importance of mutual respect, communication, and partnership in building healthy, thriving relationships. Angelou would tell families *"The love of the family, the love of one person can heal. It heals the scars left by a larger society. A massive, powerful society."*

Families, once the cornerstone of Zion's strength, now find themselves torn apart by internal strife and discord. Generations of unresolved conflicts and misunderstandings have festered, eroding trust and communication between loved ones. The resulting dysfunction and disunity within households have left scars that run deep, further exacerbating the kingdom's social fabric. Children being born out of Wedlock, Divorce, and broken homes continue to plage the Kingdom.

Tupac Continues to Get Pressured

As the challenges facing the Kingdom of Zion escalate, a new threat emerges in the form of drug lords who seek to maintain their illicit operations within the kingdom's borders. Unwilling to relinquish their hold on the lucrative drug trade in Zion, these criminal elements view Tupac and the Blackstone alliance as obstacles to their continued profitability and influence.

In an audacious move, the drug lords approach Tupac with a tempting offer: a substantial bribe in exchange for allowing them to continue their nefarious activities unchecked within the kingdom. They believe that by greasing the wheels of corruption, they can ensure their illicit enterprises remain profitable and unimpeded, regardless of the toll they exact on the community.

Tupac, faced with a moral dilemma of immense proportions, finds himself at a crossroads. On one hand, the allure of easy money and the promise of short-term gain may be tempting, particularly in light of the kingdom's pressing financial needs and mounting challenges. On the other hand, Tupac understands the profound implications of accepting such a bribe, not only for the integrity of the Blackstone alliance but also for the well-being and safety of the people of Zion.

Ultimately, Tupac's decision carries weighty consequences that extend far beyond his own personal gain. It will shape the future of the Kingdom of Zion and determine whether its leaders can remain true to their principles in the face of temptation and corruption. With the fate of the kingdom hanging in the balance, Tupac must weigh his options carefully and consider the long-term impact of his choices on the community he has sworn to protect and serve.

Tupac Seeks Council from Malcolm X

Seeking guidance in a moment of moral reckoning, Tupac turns to Malcolm X for counsel, recognizing the wisdom and insight that the esteemed leader can offer. In their candid conversation, Malcolm X imparts invaluable lessons on the importance of integrity and steadfastness in the face of adversity.

With a deep sense of conviction, Malcolm emphasizes the fundamental principle that true leadership is grounded in unwavering principles and moral rectitude. He reminds Tupac that the measure of a man is not found in the wealth or power he accrues, but rather in the integrity and righteousness of his actions. He made sure Tupac understood, *"A man who stands for nothing will fall for anything."*

Drawing from his own experiences and the teachings of his mentor, the Honorable Elijah Muhammad, Malcolm X underscores the inherent dangers of compromising one's principles for short-term gain. He warns Tupac of the insidious nature of corruption and the corrosive effects it can have on both individuals and communities, eroding trust, dignity, and self-respect in its wake.

With unwavering conviction, Malcolm X urges Tupac to stand firm in his commitment to justice, righteousness, and the well-being of the Kingdom of Zion. He reminds him that true leadership requires courage, resilience, and an unshakeable dedication to the greater good, even in the face of temptation and adversity.

Inspired by Malcolm X's words of wisdom, Tupac rededicates himself to the principles of integrity and righteousness that have guided him thus far. With renewed resolve, he rejects the drug lords' bribe and reaffirms his commitment to upholding the values of the Blackstone alliance and serving the people of Zion with honor, dignity, and integrity.

Zion Hits a Low Point

With newfound determination and a strengthened resolve, Tupac returns to confront the drug lords, delivering a resolute message that their corrupt offers and illicit activities have no place within the Kingdom of Zion. Unwavering in his commitment to uphold the principles of integrity and righteousness, he makes it clear that he will not compromise the safety and well-being of his people for the sake of personal gain or profit.

However, the drug lords, angered by Tupac's refusal to capitulate to their demands, respond with aggression and violence, unleashing their goons to intimidate and threaten him into submission. Despite Tupac's courage and resolve, he finds himself outnumbered and outmatched by the ruthless enforcers of the drug trade, forcing him to retreat in the face of overwhelming force.

As the weight of responsibility bears down on him and the challenges facing the Kingdom of Zion intensify, Tupac finds himself grappling with overwhelming stress and pressure. The weight of leadership, coupled with the relentless demands of confronting corruption and injustice, takes its toll on his mental and emotional well-being, leaving him feeling drained and exhausted.

In moments of solitude, Tupac wrestles with doubt and uncertainty, questioning whether he has the strength and resilience to carry on in the face of such daunting obstacles. The burden of leadership weighs heavily on his shoulders, as he shoulders the hopes and dreams of an entire community counting on him to lead them to a better future.

Big Boss Takes Over

As the Kingdom of Zion grapples with ongoing challenges, a new threat emerges in the form of a powerful drug lord named Big Boss, whose influence begins to spread like wildfire throughout the streets. With promises of wealth, power, and the illusion of the good life, Big Boss captures the imaginations of many young people in the community, drawing them into his web of corruption and violence.

Fueled by greed and desperation, a growing number of youth are seduced by Big Boss's criminal empire, seeing it as a means to escape the poverty and hardship that plague their lives. Seduced by the allure of fast money and the trappings of success, they become ensnared in a dangerous cycle of addiction, crime, and exploitation, sacrificing their futures in pursuit of fleeting riches.

As Big Boss tightens his grip on the streets of Zion, the community finds itself under siege, with drug-related violence and crime reaching alarming levels. Families are torn apart, lives are shattered, and the fabric of society begins to unravel under the weight of Big Boss's influence.

Despite the gravity of the situation, the allure of Big Boss's empire proves difficult to resist for many, as they are drawn deeper into a world of darkness and despair. With each passing day, the Kingdom of Zion finds itself teetering on the brink of collapse, its once vibrant streets now overrun by the shadow of corruption and greed.

In the face of this existential threat, the Blackstone Alliance must mobilize the community to stand against Big Boss and his criminal enterprise. They must offer hope and opportunity to those who have been led astray by Big Boss, showing them that there is a better path forward—one built on principles of integrity, justice, and solidarity.

As the battle for the soul of Zion intensifies, Tupac and his allies must confront the harsh realities of the streets, knowing that the fate of their kingdom hangs in the balance. With courage, determination, and unwavering resolve, they must rise to the challenge, united in their determination to reclaim their community from the clutches of darkness and build a future where peace, prosperity, and justice prevail.

Women of Zion Fall Back to Old Habits

As the allure of fast money and the promise of a better life grip the streets of Zion, the impact of Big Boss's influence extends beyond just the youth. In a desperate bid to escape poverty and hardship, some women in the community are drawn into the same cycle of exploitation and degradation, resorting to selling their bodies in exchange for financial gain. Many use social media as a means to perpetuate overly sexualized images of themself, causing men to stumble into lust.

Driven by a combination of economic necessity and societal pressures, these women abandon their sense of dignity and self-respect, succumbing to the allure of easy money and the false promises of material wealth. In their pursuit of financial stability, they forsake the values of modesty and virtue, adopting a more overtly sexualized appearance and behavior in a bid to attract men and secure their livelihoods.

The consequences of this descent into moral decay are profound, as the fabric of the community begins to unravel under the weight of exploitation and degradation. Families are torn apart, relationships are shattered, and the moral fiber of society is eroded by the corrosive influence of greed and desperation.

For the women of Zion, the path to redemption is fraught with obstacles and challenges, as they struggle to reclaim their dignity and self-worth in the face of overwhelming temptation and societal pressure. Yet, amidst the darkness and despair, there remains a glimmer of hope—a chance for redemption and renewal, guided by the principles of compassion, empathy, and solidarity.

As the Blackstone Alliance confront the scourge of exploitation and degradation within their community, they must also address the root causes of this moral decay, offering support and resources to those who have fallen victim to the allure of fast money and the false promises of material wealth. Through education, empowerment, and advocacy, they seek to uplift and empower the women of Zion, guiding them towards a path of healing, dignity, and self-respect.

In the face of adversity, the Blackstone Alliance remain steadfast in their commitment to building a better future for the Kingdom of Zion, one grounded in principles of justice, equality, and compassion. With unity, determination, and unwavering resolve, they confront the challenges before them, knowing that the strength of their community lies in the resilience and compassion of its people.

Poor Habits are Causing People's Health to Decline

As the Kingdom of Zion grapples with various social and economic challenges, another insidious threat looms on the horizon: the deteriorating health of its people due to years of poor eating habits. The pervasive influence of junk food, fast food, and unhealthy dietary choices has taken a significant toll on the physical well-being of the community, leading to a rise in chronic diseases, obesity, and overall decline in health.

For generations, the people of Zion have been inundated with a steady diet of greasy fried foods, sugary snacks, and processed foods laden with preservatives and artificial ingredients. These dietary habits, coupled with a lack of access to fresh, nutritious foods, have contributed to a growing epidemic of lifestyle-related illnesses such as diabetes, cancer, heart disease, and hypertension.

Furthermore, the consumption of unclean foods like pork and shrimp, prohibited by the Lord in the Bible, further exacerbates the health crisis within the community. Despite warnings about the health risks associated with these dietary choices, many continue to indulge in these forbidden foods, unaware of the long-term consequences for their health and well-being.

As a result, the Kingdom of Zion finds itself facing a public health crisis of unprecedented proportions, with an increasing number of its citizens suffering from preventable illnesses and health complications. Families are torn apart by chronic diseases, healthcare costs skyrocket, and the overall quality of life diminishes as the burden of poor health weighs heavily on the community.

In the face of this dire situation, the Blackstone alliance recognize the urgent need to address the root causes of poor nutrition and unhealthy dietary habits within the Kingdom of Zion. They launch a comprehensive public health campaign aimed at raising awareness about the importance of healthy eating, promoting access to fresh, nutritious foods, and advocating for policies that support community health and wellness.

Through education, outreach, and community engagement, the Blackstone Alliance must empower the people of Zion to make healthier choices for themselves and their families, providing resources and support to help them adopt sustainable lifestyle changes. They emphasize the importance of returning to traditional dietary practices rooted in whole, unprocessed foods, and encourage the cultivation of community gardens and urban agriculture initiatives to increase access to fresh produce.

As the Kingdom of Zion embarks on this journey towards improved health and wellness, the Blackstone alliance remain steadfast in their commitment to building a healthier, more vibrant future for their community. With determination, resilience, and a collective spirit of solidarity, they confront the challenges of poor nutrition head-on, knowing that the health and well-being of their people are paramount to the kingdom's prosperity and longevity.

The United States Government Offers Welfare

As the Kingdom of Zion grapples with its myriad challenges, including the deterioration of health and social issues, a new opportunity arises in the form of an offer from the President of the United States. In an attempt to address the pressing needs of the community and bolster its well-being, the President extends an offer of welfare and aid if the Kingdom of Zion agrees to reintegrate and once again become a part of the republic.

For some within the kingdom, this offer may seem like a lifeline—a chance to access much-needed resources and support that could alleviate the suffering and hardship that have plagued the community for far too long. The prospect of welfare and aid may offer a glimmer of hope in an otherwise bleak landscape, promising tangible assistance in addressing pressing issues such as healthcare, poverty, and unemployment.

However, for others, the offer is met with skepticism and apprehension. The history of systemic oppression and disenfranchisement endured by the people of Zion at the hands of the republic give pause to those who fear that accepting such assistance could come at the cost of their autonomy and self-determination. There are concerns about the strings attached to the aid, and whether it would truly address the root causes of the kingdom's problems or merely perpetuate a cycle of dependence.

As the Blackstone Alliance weigh their options, they carefully consider the potential ramifications of accepting the President's offer. They must weigh the immediate benefits of welfare and aid against the long-term implications for the kingdom's sovereignty and independence. They must also consider the desires and aspirations of the people they serve, ensuring that any decision made is in the best interests of the community as a whole.

Ultimately, the decision whether to return to the republic or maintain their autonomy lies in the hands of the people of Zion, guided by the leadership of Tupac and the Blackstone Alliance. Whatever path they choose, it will require courage, wisdom, and unity to navigate the complex challenges ahead and build a future of peace, prosperity, and justice for all.

The People of Zion are Divided

As the people of Zion engage in spirited debate over the fate of their community, differing perspectives emerge regarding the path forward. Some advocate for reintegration into the United States, seeing it as an opportunity to access much-needed resources and support that could address pressing issues such as poverty, healthcare, and education. They believe that returning to the republic offers a chance for stability and prosperity, albeit at the potential cost of autonomy and self-determination.

On the other hand, there are those who staunchly oppose reintegration, preferring to maintain the sovereignty and independence of the Kingdom of Zion under the leadership of the Blackstone alliance. They argue that remaining autonomous allows the community to preserve its unique identity, culture, and values, free from external interference and influence. They believe in the principles of self-reliance and self-governance, prioritizing the empowerment and agency of the people of Zion above all else.

As the debate unfolds, tensions rise and emotions run high, reflecting the deeply held convictions and aspirations of the people of Zion. Each side presents compelling arguments and draws upon their own lived experiences and perspectives to make their case. Some fear that returning to the republic would erode the hard-fought gains and sacrifices made by the Blackstone alliance, while others see it as a pragmatic solution to the kingdom's immediate challenges.

Amidst the discord and uncertainty, the Blackstone alliance find themselves at a crossroads, tasked with guiding their community through this pivotal moment in its history. They must navigate the complexities of the debate with wisdom, empathy, and leadership, ensuring that the voices of all stakeholders are heard and respected. Ultimately, the decision whether to return to the republic or maintain autonomy rests with the collective will of the people of Zion, who must come together to chart a path forward that reflects their shared values, aspirations, and vision for the future.

Martin Luther King Jr. Turns to the Bible for Answers

Inspired by the timeless wisdom of scripture, Martin Luther King Jr. turns to the pages of the Bible in search of guidance and solace amidst the tumultuous debates and divisions plaguing the Kingdom of Zion. As he reads the words of 2 Chronicles 7:14 "If my people, which are called by my name, shall humble themselves, and pray, and seek my face, and turn from their wicked ways; then will I hear from heaven, and will forgive their sin, and will heal their land", a profound realization dawns upon him—that true peace and healing can only come through humility, prayer, and repentance.

With a heavy heart and a burdened spirit, Martin Luther King Jr. shares his revelation with Tupac, emphasizing the importance of spiritual renewal and moral awakening as essential prerequisites for lasting peace and prosperity. He reflects on the deep-seated issues of pride, selfishness, and moral decay that have plagued the community, recognizing that true transformation can only occur when the people of Zion humble themselves before God and turn away from their sinful ways.

Together, Martin Luther King Jr. and Tupac contemplate the implications of this profound truth, grappling with the complexities of human nature and the challenges of fostering genuine repentance and reconciliation within the community. They recognize that achieving true peace and healing will require a collective effort—a willingness on the part of every individual to acknowledge their shortcomings, seek forgiveness, and commit to a path of righteousness and redemption.

Moved by the urgency of the moment and the promise of divine intervention, Martin Luther King Jr. and Tupac resolve to lead by example, embodying the principles of humility, prayer, and repentance in their own lives and encouraging others to do the same. They recognize that the journey toward healing and reconciliation will be arduous and fraught with challenges, but they remain steadfast in their belief that with faith and perseverance, the people of Zion can overcome adversity and forge a brighter future for themselves and generations to come.

As they embark on this spiritual journey of self-discovery and renewal, Martin Luther King Jr. and Tupac draw strength from the timeless teachings of scripture, knowing that in humility and faith, there is hope for healing, forgiveness, and reconciliation. With hearts open to Christ and minds attuned to the call of conscience, they set forth on a path of transformation, trusting in the promise of divine grace to guide them toward a future of peace, justice, and reconciliation in the Kingdom of Zion.

Martin Luther King Gives a Speech

Amidst the turmoil and uncertainty gripping the Kingdom of Zion, Martin Luther King Jr. emerges as a beacon of hope and inspiration, carrying with him a message of redemption, resilience, and renewal. With characteristic eloquence and passion, he takes to the podium, rallying the people with one of his powerful speeches, stirring their hearts and igniting a spark of hope within their souls. His speech is called "My New Dream Will Never Die".

As the echoes of his words reverberate through the streets of Zion, a palpable sense of pride and determination washes over the crowd, infusing them with a renewed sense of purpose and resolve. They are moved by Martin Luther King Jr.'s message of humility, prayer, and repentance, recognizing the importance of addressing their collective shortcomings and working towards a brighter future for their community.

In a moment of clarity and unity, the people of Zion overwhelmingly reject the offer of the United States president, choosing instead to stand firm in their commitment to autonomy and self-determination. They recognize that true peace and prosperity can only be achieved through internal transformation and collective action, and they are willing to rise to the challenge, confronting their issues head-on with courage and conviction.

With renewed resolve and a sense of collective purpose, the people of Zion pledge to work together to address the root causes of their challenges, embracing the principles of humility, prayer, and repentance as guiding values on their journey towards healing and reconciliation. They understand that the road ahead will be fraught with challenges, but they are undeterred, knowing that with faith, perseverance, and unity, they can overcome any obstacle and build a future of peace, justice, and prosperity for generations to come.

As they stand united in their determination to chart their own course, free from external influence and interference, the people of Zion take a bold step forward, embarking on a journey of self-discovery, empowerment, and transformation. With Martin Luther King Jr. leading the way, they march forward with hope in their hearts, knowing that the power to shape their destiny lies within their hands.

Bob Marley Meets with Martin Luther King Jr.

In a profound meeting of minds and spirits, Bob Marley and Martin Luther King Jr. come together to discuss the future of the Kingdom of Zion and the pivotal role that faith and spirituality play in guiding its people towards healing and renewal. In the majestic halls of the Castle, where the echoes of history intertwine with the whispers of the present, the grand corridors adorned with symbols of strength and resilience, they are drawn to a quiet chamber where they can speak freely and openly about the future of the Kingdom of Zion. They share a deep sense of purpose and conviction, united in their commitment to bring the people of Zion back to the ways of Jah.

Bob Marley, with his unwavering faith and deep reverence for the teachings of the Bible, understands the transformative power of Jah's message and its potential to inspire and uplift the hearts and souls of the people. With humility and reverence, he expresses his heartfelt dedication to supporting Martin Luther King Jr. in his mission to lead the people of Zion towards spiritual renewal and redemption.

As they delve into the scriptures and reflect on the timeless wisdom contained within, Bob Marley and Martin Luther King Jr. find solace and guidance in the teachings of Jah, drawing strength from its message of love, compassion, and unity. They recognize that true healing and transformation can only come through a deep and abiding connection to the divine, and they commit themselves wholeheartedly to sharing Jah's message with the people of Zion.

Together, Bob Marley and Martin Luther King Jr. pledge to work hand in hand, bridging the divide between faith and activism, and guiding the people of Zion towards a future of peace, justice, and spiritual fulfillment. With humility, grace, and unwavering faith in the power of Jah's love, they set forth on a journey of enlightenment and empowerment, knowing that with faith and perseverance, all things are possible.

As they part ways, Bob Marley and Martin Luther King Jr. carry with them a renewed sense of purpose and determination, inspired by the timeless truths of Jah's message and empowered by the strength of their collective spirit. With hearts open to God and minds attuned to the call of conscience, they set forth on a path of transformation, guided by the light of Jah's love and the promise of a brighter tomorrow for the Kingdom of Zion.

Bob Marley Talks to the Youth of the Kingdom

In a powerful demonstration of his unwavering commitment to the well-being of the Kingdom of Zion, Bob Marley turns his attention to the youth, recognizing them as the future guardians of Zion and the torchbearers of love, compassion, and unity. With humility and grace, he reaches out to the young hearts and minds of the community, inviting them to embrace the timeless values and principles that lie at the heart of Jah's teachings.

With a gentle spirit and an infectious passion for righteousness, Bob Marley imparts his wisdom and knowledge to the youth, guiding them on a journey of self-discovery and spiritual enlightenment. He speaks to them of the importance of love and compassion for their brothers and sisters, urging them to embrace the inherent dignity and worth of every soul, regardless of race, creed, or background.

Drawing upon the rich tapestry of Biblical truths and philosophy, Bob Marley shares with the youth the profound teachings of Jah, inviting them to cultivate a deep and abiding connection to the divine and to seek solace and guidance in the eternal truths that lie within. He speaks of the importance of humility, gratitude, and reverence for the natural world, instilling in the young hearts a sense of reverence and awe for the beauty and majesty of creation.

As the youth listen intently to Bob Marley's words, their hearts are stirred, and their spirits are uplifted, as they feel the transformative power of Jah's love coursing through their veins. They are inspired to live lives of purpose and meaning, guided by the principles of righteousness and justice, and fueled by the fire of compassion and empathy for their fellow human beings. He speaks to them about the destructive impact of drugs and violence and the importance of building a better future for themselves and their families.

Through community outreach programs, workshops, and educational initiatives, Bob Marley works tirelessly to empower youth with the tools and resources they need to resist the allure of drugs and violence and chart a course toward a brighter tomorrow. He instills in them a sense of pride in their cultural heritage and identity, fostering a spirit of unity and solidarity that transcends boundaries and divisions. He expresses to them, *"We know where we're going. We know where we're from. We're leaving*

Babylon. We're going to our father land. Exodus! Movement of Jah people, oh yeah!"

As Bob Marley's message of peace and love resonates throughout the community, a groundswell of support emerges, uniting residents in their shared commitment to building a safer, more prosperous future for the Kingdom of Zion. With Bob Marley as their guide and mentor, the youth of the Kingdom of Zion embark on a journey of self-discovery and spiritual growth, embracing the values and principles that will shape their destinies and guide them towards a future of peace, harmony, and spiritual fulfillment. Together, they stand united in their commitment to Jah's message, as they strive to build a world where love, compassion, and unity reign supreme, now and for generations to come.

Maya Angelou Writes a Constitution

In a momentous display of wisdom and vision, Maya Angelou, the esteemed poet and sage of the Kingdom of Zion, takes pen to paper to craft a constitution that will serve as the bedrock of the nation's governance and the embodiment of its values and aspirations. With a profound understanding of human nature and a deep reverence for justice and equality, Maya Angelou channels her unparalleled eloquence and insight into a document that will shape the destiny of the Kingdom of Zion for generations to come.

Drawing inspiration from the timeless principles of love, compassion, and unity, Maya Angelou weaves together a tapestry of rights, freedoms, and responsibilities that reflect the inherent dignity and worth of every soul. In her constitution, she enshrines the principles of equality before the law, freedom of expression, and the protection of fundamental human rights, ensuring that every citizen of the Kingdom of Zion is treated with dignity, respect, and fairness under the law.

But Maya Angelou's constitution goes beyond mere legal provisions; it is a testament to the values and aspirations that define the soul of the Kingdom of Zion. With her characteristic grace and eloquence, she articulates a vision of a society where justice reigns supreme, where the marginalized and oppressed are uplifted and empowered, and where the pursuit of truth, beauty, and wisdom is celebrated as the highest expression of human potential.

As the ink dries on the parchment and the words of Maya Angelou's constitution echo through the halls of power, the Kingdom of Zion is set to rise—a beacon of hope and inspiration in a world in need of healing and renewal. Guided by the timeless principles of

love, compassion, and unity, the people of Zion embark on a journey towards a future of peace, prosperity, and justice for all, knowing that their constitution will serve as a guiding light and a testament to the enduring power of the human spirit. Constitution begins with the words *"You may write me down in history, with your bitter, twisted lies, You may trod me in the very dirt, But still, like dust, I'll rise."*

Whitney Houston Develops the National Flag

Whitney Houston, ever the visionary, unveils a powerful symbol of unity and resilience for the Kingdom of Zion—the newly designed flag. With a bold design that speaks to the essence of the community, the flag features a striking combination of colors and symbols that embody the spirit of the people.

At its core is a radiant gold circle, representing the rising sun—a symbol of hope, renewal, and enlightenment. Surrounding the circle, a vibrant red swath symbolizes the blood shed by martyrs and the fiery passion that burns within the hearts of the people. Below, a deep black field represents the diverse shades of the community, united in their shared identity and strength.

Together, these elements come together to form a powerful emblem of the Kingdom's journey from darkness to light, from struggle to triumph. As the flag flies high above the Kingdom of Zion, it serves as a beacon of hope and inspiration, reminding all who see it of the resilience, unity, and unwavering spirit of its people.

Tupac and Malcolm X Decide How to Take on Big Boss

In a tense yet determined meeting, Malcolm X and Tupac come together to devise a strategic plan to confront the formidable threat posed by Big Boss and his criminal empire. With a keen understanding of the stakes and the challenges ahead, they deliberate on the best course of action, drawing upon their respective strengths and experiences to chart a path towards victory for the Kingdom of Zion.

Malcolm X, with his sharp intellect and unwavering commitment to justice, emphasizes the importance of organizing the community and mobilizing grassroots support to challenge Big Boss's stranglehold on power. He advocates for a multifaceted approach that combines peaceful resistance with targeted activism, leveraging the power of collective action to weaken Big Boss's influence and dismantle his criminal network from within.

Tupac, with his charisma and streetwise savvy, stresses the need for bold and decisive action to confront Big Boss head-on. He proposes a more aggressive strategy that involves rallying a formidable force to directly challenge Big Boss and his henchmen, employing both tactical prowess and sheer force of will to overcome their adversaries and reclaim control of the streets.

As they weigh the pros and cons of their respective approaches, Malcolm X and Tupac find common ground in their shared goal of liberating the Kingdom of Zion from the grip of tyranny and oppression. They recognize that their strengths complement each other, and that by combining their efforts, they can create a powerful synergy that will be impossible for Big Boss to ignore.

With a renewed sense of purpose and solidarity, Malcolm X and Tupac forge a strategic alliance, pledging to work together to mobilize the people of Zion and confront Big Boss with a unified front. They recognize that the road ahead will be fraught with challenges and dangers, but they are undeterred, knowing that the cause they fight for is just and righteous. Malcolm X glares at Tupac and insists, *"If you're not ready to die for it, put the word 'freedom' out of your vocabulary."*

Armed with a clear plan of action and a steadfast commitment to their cause, Malcolm X and Tupac set out to mobilize their forces and prepare for the decisive showdown with Big Boss and his criminal empire. With courage in their hearts and justice on their side, they stand ready to confront whatever obstacles may lie in their path, confident that together, they can overcome any challenge and secure a brighter future for the Kingdom of Zion.

Tupac and Malcolm X Meet with the Men of the Kingdom

Gathered in a solemn assembly, Tupac and Malcolm X sit with the men of the Kingdom of Zion, their faces etched with determination and resolve. With unwavering conviction, they lay out their plan to confront the scourge of corruption and violence that has plagued their streets, rallying the men to take a stand and reclaim their community from the clutches of Big Boss and his criminal empire.

As the men of the kingdom listen intently to Tupac and Malcolm X's impassioned plea, a sense of unity and purpose fills the air. They understand the gravity of the situation and the importance of their role in bringing about change. With a collective sense of responsibility, they pledge their allegiance to the cause, vowing to keep the streets clean and to stand together in solidarity against the forces of injustice and oppression.

With heads held high and hearts afire with determination, the men of the Kingdom of Zion take a solemn oath to uphold the values of righteousness, integrity, and courage. They pledge to work tirelessly alongside Tupac and Malcolm X to rid their streets of corruption and violence, and to create a safer and more prosperous future for themselves and their families.

With the strength of their unity and the power of their collective resolve, Tupac, Malcolm X, and the men of the Kingdom of Zion set out to confront Big Boss and his criminal empire head-on. Armed with the oath they have sworn and the unwavering support of their community, they march forward with courage and determination, knowing that together, they can overcome any obstacle and bring about the change they so desperately seek.

Big Boss Leaves Town

As the pressure mounts and the tide of community support turns against him, Big Boss finds himself facing an insurmountable challenge in the Kingdom of Zion. With the combined efforts of Tupac, Malcolm X, and the determined citizens of Zion, his grip on power begins to slip, and the once impenetrable fortress of his criminal empire crumbles before his very eyes.

Faced with the overwhelming force of justice and righteousness, Big Boss realizes that he can no longer maintain his stronghold in the Kingdom of Zion. With no other recourse available to him, he makes the difficult decision to retreat, knowing that he has been defeated by the collective will of the people and the indomitable spirit of unity that has taken root in Zion.

With a heavy heart and a sense of resignation, Big Boss gathers his remaining loyalists and makes plans to leave the Kingdom of Zion behind. Recognizing that his reign of terror has come to an end, he sets his sights on a new horizon, seeking refuge in the bustling streets of Detroit, where he hopes to rebuild his criminal empire from the ground up.

As Big Boss makes his hasty departure from Zion, the streets erupt in celebration, as the citizens rejoice in their hard-fought victory over tyranny and oppression. With a newfound sense of freedom and hope, they look towards the future with optimism and determination, knowing that they have overcome adversity and emerged stronger and more united than ever before.

Though Big Boss may have fled to Detroit, his legacy of corruption and violence is soon forgotten in the Kingdom of Zion, as the community comes together to rebuild and renew their streets. With Tupac, Malcolm X, and the unwavering support of the people at the helm, Zion begins a new chapter in its history—a chapter defined by justice, equality, and the triumph of good over evil.

Whitney Houston Teaches Young Women

With a heart full of compassion and a deep understanding of the struggles faced by young women in the Kingdom of Zion, Whitney Houston takes on the important task of empowering and uplifting her fellow sisters. Drawing upon her own experiences and wisdom gained over a lifetime in the spotlight, she reaches out to teen moms and those who have turned to selling their bodies, offering them guidance, support, and a path towards healing and redemption.

In her role as a mentor and advocate, Whitney Houston teaches young women the importance of self-respect and self-worth, instilling in them a sense of dignity and pride in who they are. She emphasizes the value of inner beauty and strength, encouraging them to embrace their unique gifts and talents, and to never compromise their integrity for the sake of fleeting pleasures or external validation.

With compassion and empathy, Whitney Houston sits down with teen moms and those who have struggled with selling their bodies, offering them a listening ear and a shoulder to lean on. She shares her own journey of overcoming adversity and finding redemption, inspiring them to believe in themselves and to recognize their inherent worth as daughters of Zion.

Through her words and actions, Whitney Houston imparts invaluable lessons of resilience, self-love, and forgiveness, encouraging young women to learn from their past mistakes and to chart a new course for their future. She teaches them the importance of making positive choices and surrounding themselves with supportive and uplifting influences, as they strive to create a life of purpose, fulfillment, and dignity.

As Whitney Houston walks alongside these young women on their journey of self-discovery and empowerment, she serves as a beacon of hope and inspiration, reminding them that no matter how difficult their circumstances may be, they have the strength and courage to rise above their challenges and to create a life of beauty, joy, and meaning. Through her love and guidance, she helps to heal the wounds of the past and to pave the way for a brighter and more promising future for all. She tells them that *"I decided long ago, never to walk in anyone's shadows. If I fail, if I succeed...At least I live as I believe. No matter what they take from me, They can't take away my dignity. Because the greatest love of all is happening to me. I found the greatest love of all inside of me. The greatest*

love of all is easy to achieve. Learning to LOVE Yourself...It is the GREATEST love of all".

The Blackstone Alliance Restore Order

With the triumphant victory of the Blackstone Alliance, order and prosperity are restored to the Kingdom of Zion. Through their unwavering commitment to justice and unity, Tupac, Malcolm X, and their esteemed allies have succeeded in creating a thriving community where peace, productivity, and righteousness reign supreme.

Under the wise and compassionate leadership of the Blackstone Alliance, the people of Zion experience a newfound sense of hope and optimism for the future. Freed from the shackles of oppression and corruption, they embrace their roles as active participants in building a brighter and more equitable society for all.

With the streets cleaned of crime and violence, the citizens of Zion are free to pursue their dreams and aspirations with renewed vigor and determination. Businesses flourish, schools thrive, and families prosper, as the economy booms and opportunities abound for all who call Zion home.

But perhaps most importantly, the people of Zion are living righteous lives, guided by the timeless principles of love, compassion, and justice. Inspired by the example set forth by the Blackstone Alliance, they strive to uphold these values in all aspects of their daily lives, treating one another with kindness and respect, and working together towards the common good.

As the Kingdom of Zion enters a new era of peace and prosperity, the legacy of the Blackstone Alliance lives on as a testament to the power of unity, courage, and righteous action. Through their leadership and sacrifice, Tupac, Malcolm X, Bob Marley, Whitney Houston, Maya Angelou, and Martin Luther King Jr. have not only restored order to Zion but have paved the way for a future filled with hope, opportunity, and boundless potential for all who dwell within its borders and everywhere.

The President of the United States is Not Happy

As the Kingdom of Zion basks in the glow of its newfound peace and prosperity, a dark cloud looms on the horizon in the form of the President of the United States. Despite the happiness and contentment of the people of Zion, the president's dissatisfaction with their rejection of his offer to rejoin the republic simmers beneath the surface, fueling his desire to assert control over the independent nation.

Feeling slighted by Zion's refusal to acquiesce to his demands, the president becomes increasingly agitated and resentful, viewing the thriving kingdom as a thorn in the side of the United States' hegemony. In his eyes, Zion's rejection of his offer represents a challenge to his authority and a threat to the stability of the region, prompting him to consider drastic measures to assert his dominance.

With a sense of entitlement and hubris, the president begins to entertain the idea of invading Zion, viewing it as a necessary step to bring the renegade nation back under his control. Ignoring the cries for peace and diplomacy, he opts for a path of aggression and coercion, determined to bend Zion to his will through force if necessary.

As tensions escalate between the United States and the Kingdom of Zion, the people of Zion brace themselves for the looming threat of invasion, unwilling to compromise their hard-won independence and sovereignty. With the Blackstone Alliance at their helm, they stand united in their determination to defend their homeland against any who would seek to subjugate them.

But even as the drums of war beat louder and the specter of conflict looms ever closer, the people of Zion remain resolute in their commitment to peace and righteousness. With unwavering faith in their cause and the strength of their unity, they stand ready to face whatever challenges may come their way, confident that justice will prevail and the Kingdom of Zion will endure, no matter the odds.

Tupac and Whitney Houston Become Close

While Tupac stands at the helm of the Kingdom of Zion, leading with courage and determination, there is a notable absence by his side—a void that whispers of longing and unspoken desires. Despite his unwavering commitment to the people of Zion and his tireless efforts to uplift and empower his community, Tupac cannot shake the feeling of loneliness that gnaws at his heart.

But as the days pass and the responsibilities of leadership weigh ever heavier upon him, Tupac struggles to find someone who can fill the void in his heart. He searches for a queen who embodies the virtues of strength, wisdom, and compassion—a woman who shares his vision for a better world and is willing to stand by his side as they work together to make that vision a reality.

As Tupac and Whitney Houston collaborate closely in the Kingdom of Zion, a deep and undeniable connection begins to form between them. Beyond their shared commitment to the community and their mutual admiration for each other's courage and resilience, there is a simmering undercurrent of attraction that neither can ignore.

In quiet moments, as they work side by side, Tupac and Whitney find themselves drawn to each other's presence, their conversations lingering a little longer, their gazes lingering a little deeper. They share intimate moments of vulnerability and authenticity, opening up to each other in ways they never thought possible.

Tupac is captivated by Whitney's beauty, grace, and inner strength, drawn to the warmth and compassion that radiates from her soul. He finds himself mesmerized by her presence, unable to shake the feeling that she holds a special place in his heart.

Similarly, Whitney is drawn to Tupac's magnetic charisma, his passion, and his unwavering commitment to justice. She admires his strength and resilience, and feels a deep sense of connection with him that transcends words.

As their bond deepens, Tupac and Whitney find themselves irresistibly drawn to each other, their hearts entwined in a dance of longing and desire. Though they may try to deny their feelings or push them aside, the attraction between them only grows stronger with each passing day, until it becomes impossible to ignore.

Despite the undeniable chemistry and mutual admiration that exists between them, Tupac and Whitney ultimately decide to prioritize their responsibilities to the Kingdom of Zion above their own personal desires. They choose to exercise restraint and caution, knowing that their commitment to the greater good must take precedence over their individual happiness. Or will it?...

To Be Continued…